THE
COME ON

THE
COME ON

A NOVEL OF SUSPENSE

JIM CIRNI

SOHO

Copyright © 1989 by James N. Cirnigliaro.
All rights reserved under International and Pan-American Copyright
Conventions.
Published in the United States of America by
Soho Press, Inc.
1 Union Square
New York, N.Y. 10003
Library of Congress Cataloging-in-Publication Data

Cirni, Jim 1937–
The come on.

I. Title.
PS3553.I76C6   1989   813'.54   89-6269
ISBN 0-939149-24-9

Manufactured in the United States
First Edition

For my mother, Jennie

THE
COME ON

1

When I opened my eyes the sun was shining, a tiny sun no bigger than a pinpoint. Which for some odd reason was jumping around like the bouncing ball in the old sing-along cartoons. My first thought was universal catastrophe. Planet Earth had slipped out of orbit.

I tried closing my eyes to the light but something held them open. Thumbs.

"Told you he ain't dead," came a voice from beyond the sun.

"Looks dead," said another voice.

"Nah," came a third. "See the eyes?

They're movin' in and out."

"They're dilatin', stupid."

"That means he's dead, don't it?"

The penlight vanished. I drifted peacefully, contemplating

3

my life and the love of my older brother James, which had brought me to this impasse.

James had a lucrative law practice in Akron and I had been unemployed and broke in Queens. It seemed only natural to ask him for help.

"Jesus, Fran," he said, the day I called to fill him in on the deal. "You've got an accounting degree. Use the damn thing!"

I sighed. "I know, I know. I could've been a comptroller."

"You sound like Marlon Brando," he said.

"I'm a bartender, James. Or I was until recently. That's why I want to borrow the money. To open a place of my own."

"For *three* hundred thousand dollars? I'm a lawyer, not an arbitrager."

"So lend me what you can. We'll sign notes for the balance. It's a great spot. Ten minutes from where I live. Trust me, James."

I have to admit that I took my brother's money under false pretenses. Oh, I opened the restaurant, all right. It just wasn't what James had in mind. He wanted a "family" restaurant but the families who packed the place didn't come from the suburbs, or include kids, or show up on holidays with grandma and grandpa for the senior citizens discount. The klans that patronized my place were somewhat more notorious, and all of them were rubbing shoulders on neutral turf—my turf.

There was no simple way to convince James out in Akron that none of this had been done by design. He'd never understand that in the Queens, New York bar scene big spenders are like women who track their favorite hairdresser from shop to shop. What I'm saying is, a bartender has his own following.

For seven years I'd been punching a register for someone else, pouring drinks six nights a week for $300 plus tips. I knew straights by their surname, cheaters by their sobriquet, and wiseguys by their monicker. I knew when to talk and when to go mute, when to look and when to turn away. I'd seen guns, knives, drugs, threats, fights, and once—only once, thank God—an actual murder. And though all of this would look unseemly on a resume, it had given me a certain reputation.

I figured all it would take to get the place off the ground was a good chef and a staff that wouldn't rob me blind. I didn't count on the kind of success that comes with a high rolling clientele. Mr. Prosperity had moved in with Lady Luck. For thirty-eight years I'd wondered where the hell she was hiding. Unfortunately, she had Mr. Scarlo on her other arm.

This particular night some bimbo had tried to flush a tampon into the East River. It hadn't quite made it. There wasn't time to call a plumber so the boss was dealing with it himself. Or trying to. I was sweating over a hot plunger when Sally Plunk floated in.

"Face it, Fontana," she said. "Mr. Goodwrench you ain't."

"Yeah," I said. "Donald Duck would be more like it. I want a sign on the wall, Sally."

"Won't do any good." She said it with a smirk. "The one's who come in here can't read. Speaking of which, Scarlo's outside, with three ladies and his usual associates."

"Siddown, siddown," John Scarlo said from one side of his face. Once upon a time his name had been Scarlotti. He smoked these horrible cigars that he stuffed in the corner of his mouth and even without them he couldn't talk straight.

"Wantcha to meet a class act," Scarlo told the three girls as I settled in a chair at their horse shoe booth table. Sid and Nick Petrone anchored the outside corners and two ladies flanked their patron, forming a Scarlo sandwich. The third was less enthusiastic but they had him surrounded, which was just the way he liked it.

He gave them my name then threw his arms around the two blondes on either side of him. "This is Tic," he said, gawking down at her cleavage. He nodded to the one alongside Nick. "And this one's Tac."

"Don't tell me," I said as the third blonde edged closer to Sid. "You must be Toe."

The ladies giggled and the men guffawed. I ordered a round of drinks sent over. Already I had them rolling in the aisle.

I knew Scarlo from the old days, when, as a lowly barman, I used to shave his tab, light his stogeys and make him laugh. It's what you did when you were behind the bar playing for tips. John Scarlo was a crew chief for one of the veteran heavies in Brooklyn named Manny Adonis. Scarlo excelled at two things: bragging and gambling. He had a story about every bet he'd ever made and how he had beat the odds not by luck but with an unqualified bravado he called, in Sicilian, *cucchione di ferro*. Iron balls!

To hear Scarlo tell it, you'd think he never lost a bet in his life. I made the mistake once of saying that to him in jest. What I got in response was a mini-vendetta that manifested itself in frequent smacks to the back of my head. Since then I'd moved up in class: I owned my own place—Fontana's. And Big John was a regular.

As usual, Scarlo had arrived well after midnight with his flunkies and the trio of featherheads they'd scored in some joint on the Upper Eastside. Guys like that bounced for hours before they finally settled down to feed. So it was normal to keep the kitchen open until at least two in the morning.

It had taken a while for the staff to get used to it. They bitched at first, especially the prima donnas, my chefs, who were more independent than five-hundred-dollar hookers at a Shriner's convention. I thought I'd never hold a quality chef. Then the money began to fly and it all changed. Chefs were calling me from as far away as Phoenix, Arizona.

Twenty-eight tables and two corner booths spread out over three thousand square feet of hardwood floor. I would have jammed in a few more tables, but our patrons liked their privacy. Our seating arrangement followed a strict pecking order. During prime time the two booths were strictly reserved for the creme de la crime, the dons. No one was more aware of this than Johnny Scarlo. Which is another reason he liked to come in late.

Like all *caporegime,* he was loyal to his man, but the burning desire to move up was like the eternal flame at Arlington. Scarlo was no different. He'd never miss an opportunity and taking the boss's booth when the boss wasn't there was one small step in that direction. Tonight there were six in the group and me. We sparred for a while. They ordered the special, calamari with hot sauce. We had another drink. Then the talk turned to sports. Baseball, in particular the New York Yankees. Scarlo bet them every day. He bet on other teams and other events, but mostly he lived and died with Steinbrenner's boys.

"I was just telling these little lovelies how I banged out Bobby Chubbs today," he was saying. Bobby Chubbs was a bookmaker, who wined and dined at Fontana's. Weekends Bobby took in as much as I did.

"That fucking Mattingly is unreal," Scarlo announced. "Two out in the ninth and he creams one off some *gadrool* they bring in from the bullpen. Shoulda seen it, Frankie. Fuckin' beautiful. An upper deck job." He shrugged. "But whataya expect against Cleveland, eh?"

Scarlo knew how I felt about my homestate ball club. They hadn't won a pennant in over thirty years, yet I'd loved 'em since I was a kid. Scarlo was putting the wood to that feeling and I didn't like it.

"There ain't no worse team in sports than those Indians," he said. "They're so friggin' bad I gotta give two or three runs every time they come into town."

"You're from Cleveland, aintcha, Frank?" said Sid Petrone. His pocked face had cracked into a disapproving smile.

"Akron," I said.

"Akron!" said brother Nick. "That makes a world'a difference. I hear they make rubbers in Akron, Frankie. Whatdaya do for laughs, punch holes in 'em?"

"That's cute, Nick. Actually, we diddle the homecoming queens."

"He's gettin' pissed, girls," Scarlo said. "You can always tell when Frankie's pissed. He comes on like Joe College."

"Oh," Miss Tick said. "You went to college? I had a cousin went to college."

"As what?" said Nick. "The school pump?"

It went like that until the food arrived: the brothers Petrone insulting the three dames, and Scarlo belittling the Indians. "Well," I said, getting up, "here's my cue to leave. Enjoy your meal. But watch the sauce. It's a killer."

"Ain't we all," Nick said, once again pleased by his own wit.

Scarlo stared up at me. "Stay awhile, Frank. It ain't every night the girls get to talk with a big restauranteer." He jerked a finger at me. "Come on, stick around."

I tried to beg off but Scarlo had that look in his eye. He wasn't through ragging me. I sat down.

"Pass the cheese, will ya, Sid. Frankie's gonna tell us how good the Indians are."

I shrugged. "They're not bad."

"Not bad! Those humps couldn't beat the Rockettes. Tell you what," he said. He hesitated a moment while he figured out what the "what" was going to be.

8

"There's a double-header tomorrow," he sneered. "I'll bet you a hundred bucks the Yankees beat 'em both games."

"They probably will," I said.

" '*Probably* will,'" he mimicked, then gazed over at Ms. Toe. "How do you get a rise outta this guy?"

She smiled wistfully. "Oh, there are ways."

I knew before she had finished that it was the wrong thing to say. Scarlo's face went dark. "You're with me," he said. "Remember?"

She blanched and studied her fork like she'd never seen one in her life. That's the way it was with Johnny Scarlo. One wrong word and your whole life slipped its axis.

"How about it, Frank? You up for it?"

I sighed. "Give me a break, will you, John? You know I can't gamble around here. With my luck I'd lose the place in a week."

"A friendly bet, for Chrissake. Tell you what. Forget the C-note. We'll have some fun, eh?"

Scarlo's version of fun was putting a rattlesnake in some kid's lunchbox. I knew it but I had no choice. You never do with guys like this.

"All right," I said. "Let's hear it."

"Way to go. I'll put some hair on your ass yet, don't you worry."

But I was worried. I liked my ass the way it was—white, bald, and perfectly symetrical.

"I'll give you five runs a game," he said. "I win, you blow all of us to a meal and a bottle of your best vino."

"And if I win?"

This cracked him up. The Petrones, too. The three of them carried on like the squid was still alive, wriggling and tickling the life out of them. I wasn't amused. But it would have been rude to walk away. So I watched with moderate interest, hoping the hot sauce would live up to its reputation.

When the laughing finally stopped, Scarlo squinted, raised his butter knife and pointed it at me. "If you win," he said, "let's see . . . if you win . . . shit, I don't know. I'll surprise you. How's that, Frankie? And don't sweat it, it'll be worth a helluva lot more than a freebee in this joint."

He held out his hand. "Is it a bet?"

"Bet," I said.

2

Her name was Tina Webb. She was a cop. I'd picked up with Tina shortly after my ex-wife left my life. Tina was good at putting people away. She was even better at putting paint on canvas: an aspiring artist on the verge of making a name for herself. A one-woman show at P.S. 1 led to an offer of shows in Europe and Japan. The opportunity was serious and there was no way I'd let her pass it by on my account.

We parted friends. My going away gift to Tina was the promise never to see my ex-wife again. Tina's gift to me was something more tangible. Her studio.

At the time I was closing the deal on the restaurant and sharing with Tina a swanky apartment in East Hollywood, a/k/a Astoria, Queens. The apartment was close enough to the restaurant but it wasn't where I wanted to live. Not for fourteen hundred a month, anyway.

The studio was really a loft in a rehabbed warehouse in Long Island City that she was sharing with two other girls, artists with less talent but no less desire. Their names were Emerald and Mai Ling, and they were thrilled with the notion of having a man around. Not only would I serve as their resident art critic, but as a watchdog for their equipment and works-in-process.

It wasn't a bad deal for them. I was cheaper than a dog and a lot less trouble. They'd show up on Saturday morning, whip out their stuff, work all day and leave the place in a mess. I didn't mind. Their mess rarely infringed on my own.

I had staked out the northwest corner of the studio, enclosed it in sheetrock and put in a portable closet, a small dresser, queen-size bed, twenty-one inch TV on a rolling stand, a recliner, and a coffee table on a woolen scatter rug. I put in a stall shower and added a stove and refrigerator to compliment the sink and john that were already there. You had to do the dishes in the bathroom sink, so it wasn't quite what you'd find in *Better Homes and Gardens,* but it was convenient for me.

This being Saturday, the girls arrived at eight a.m. As usual they were nauseatingly chipper, filled with enthusiasm and eager to start. They had hired a model who was due to arrive in one hour.

"Wake up, Fido!" shouted Emerald Davis, a bubbly young creature with a dark sense of humor and skin to match. "We brought you some bagels. Mai Ling wanted to bring Alpo but we know how you love soft round things with holes in them."

Mai Ling drew back the curtain that served as the door to my corner. I closed one eye and squinted through the other. Mai Ling was all smiles, her white teeth glistening in the morning sunlight. She said, "Come on, Frank, get up. If Alfonso sees you in those shorts, he'll be too excited to pose."

"That's all I need around here," I said. "Christ!"

"It's your own fault," Mai retorted. "You wouldn't pose."

"It's bad enough I do the housework. Besides, when I get naked in front of two gorgeous females, I don't expect to come up dry. What would I tell my fans? It's degrading."

We ate the bagels with lox and cream cheese I had in the fridge. That afternoon, while Mai Ling and Emerald were oohing and aahing over the aesthetics of Alfonso's musculature, I found myself in front of the television, forsaking my responsibilities to watch the ball game. I really did want to win that bet. If nothing else, it might shut Scarlo's face for a while.

Unfortunately, the Indians were doing all they could to live up to their woeful image. They were shut out in the first game 8-0, and the second game had them down by six runs going into the ninth inning. With Ron Guidry on the mound and Phil Rizzuto on the mike, things were looking pretty good for the bad guys. But the Indians weren't dead yet. They rallied for two quick runs then loaded the bases for Thunder Thorton, a .220 hitter who, on occasion, would hit a ball two thousand feet. Guidry's next pitch landed in the bullpen. Final score 6-5 Cleveland.

"Holy cow!" cried the Scooter in the press box.

What had I won, I wondered.

The one night that Fontana's isn't heavily populated with sinister characters is Saturday. Even the punks have families and Saturday night is set aside for wives. Their hangouts were off limits to wives. Call it tradition, or an unwritten law.

I figured that was the reason for Scarlo's absence. Not that it really mattered. Knowing I had won was satisfaction enough and I felt certain that I would hear no more about the Indians from

Scarlo or the Petrones. But, ten minutes before closing, Nick Petrone walked in. He was in a foul mood and didn't care who knew it. Me in particular.

I was tending bar with Sally Plunk, something I did from time to time. It broke up my night and added a personal touch that our patrons seemed to enjoy. Nick Petrone was a double-Johnny Black. He ambled over and I set him up without asking. He took a sip, held the scotch in his mouth, then sprayed it across the bar. "What the fuck you givin' me here? Clan MacGregor?"

I took the bottle of Black off the shelf, added a fresh glass and placed them both in front of him. "Be my guest," I said.

He grumbled something I couldn't hear and poured himself a triple. Nick was a tad more bellicose than his brother. But Nick was a tad younger and, in their business, belligerence seemed to wane with longevity.

I left him alone, which didn't help. Some clown accidentally kicked the stool he was on and for a while there it seemed Sally and I would be dispensing emergency first aid instead of drinks.

It was time to break out the humor. So I cruised within range and said, "What's the matter, Nick? Have a hard day at the office?"

You'd think that after looking at these guys for so many years I'd have learned the difference between a sneer and a smile. Nick was doing something with his face but damned if I knew what it was.

"You made a mistake," he said. "A bad fucking mistake."

I wasn't sure what he meant, the comment, the scotch, or just being there in front of him. "Sorry, Nick," I said. "Just trying to lighten you up a little."

"I got a message for you," he said. "From Scarlo."

"Hey, look, if it's about the bet, tell him forget it. It was only a joke."

"Sure," Nick said. "You're a real funny guy. 'Cept me and Sid ain't laughin' too much. We took a bath today. You know why?"

"You bet the wrong teams?" I said.

"Yeah, the wrong teams. Ten wrong teams. At five bucks a pop."

Fifty grand. No wonder Nick had a bug up his ass.

"For two months we do nuthin' wrong," he said. "Then you come along with your friggin' Indians."

"It wasn't my idea, Nick."

"Yeah."

"So what's the message?"

"He told me to tell you he'll be around in a few days . . . to pay off."

The thought of facing Scarlo hung over my head like the prospect of dental work. I wasn't frightened but I wasn't looking forward to it either.

I felt certain he'd show up on Wednesday. That was the night he and his crew had their weekly sit down. They'd meet with their boss, Manny Adonis, at their social club in Greenpoint, where undoubtedly they discussed financial opportunities, profit margins and cost overrides. They'd come in after the meeting, hungry for the special: tortellini soup and soft-shell crab. It was a treat for the boys who usually scoffed it up with enough wine to float the QE 2.

But Wednesday came and Scarlo was a no-show. He remained that way until the following Tuesday, when I found him in the dining room at an unpretentious table for two in the middle of the floor. It was an hour before the dinner crowd so I wasn't surprised that no one else was around. What did surprise me was that no one was around Scarlo. I couldn't recall ever seeing him alone and he looked kind of weird by himself, twisting a cold cigar between his fingers, staring down at a Tanqueray and tonic.

I knew better than to take a seat without being asked so I went up to the table and stood across from where he was sitting. "How you doing, John?"

He looked up. Pensive, sullen. Very un-Scarlo. He nodded toward the chair in front of me and I settled in, waited.

"I'm buying," he said. "Whadaya drink?" He snapped his fingers and Joanne came over.

I ordered a light scotch and both Scarlo and I watched Joanne sashay toward the service bar in her black bodysuit and fishnet stockings, standard wear prescribed by the chauvinist pig who paid the salaries.

"Nice stuff," Scarlo said. "You try them out before you put 'em on the payroll?"

"Can't," I said. "If I did they'd wind up owning the place."

Scarlo smiled but his heart wasn't in it. He looked like a man with heavy problems.

"The Yankees dropped six out of eight," he said. "Three in a row to the Tigers, and today it's Boston."

My antennae shot up but it wasn't time to panic, yet.

He lit the cigar and blew a cloud of smoke thick enough to kick off the overhead exhaust. "About the bet," he said.

Joanne arrived with the drinks. I grabbed mine and polished it off. "Another round," I said. She gave me an odd look and walked away.

"I want you to do something for me, Frankie. It's gonna sound crazy but I want you to do it."

"Look, John, if it's about the bet, forget it, okay? It didn't mean anything."

16

"That's what *I* thought," he said. "But things have turned to shit ever since. I gotta do something. You know what I mean?"

I didn't know what he meant and I didn't want to know. I wouldn't like it no matter what it was.

"The truth is," he said, "I wasn't gonna give you a fucking thing. I was hot as a bitch then and I just didn't give a shit. But you know how it is with luck. Things go bad, you gotta pull out all the stops. Try anything, you know?"

I nodded. "Yeah, I know."

"Good. So here's what we do. You go to Atlantic City. Spend a couple days at Bally's Grand. I'll comp the whole thing and we call the bet even."

He picked up his glass and started to drink.

"Can't do it," I said.

Scarlo winced, gulped loudly and looked down into his Tanqueray like it was battery acid. "Whadaya mean you can't?"

"Come on, John, I've got a business to run. I can't leave the place for two days. Besides, it's too much. If you would have won, I'd be out a few meals and a bottle of wine. That's a lot less than you'll pay for Bally's."

He shook his head. "What's with you, Fontana? Are you stupid or you just look that way? You been around long enough to know the score. Right now I'm cold. I gotta square things away. You know what I mean?"

"So give me a few dollars and call it even."

"No. It's gotta be big to turn this around."

"Suppose I do go and your luck doesn't change. Where does that put me?"

"It ain't you, you dumb fuck. It's me! I'm superstitious. Sid and Nick want me to fuck a nigger but that ain't my style."

Any attempt to dissuade Scarlo would have been futile. And

unhealthy. There was no limit to how far these people would go to appease their superstitions. Scarlo had once pushed his brand new Seville off the pier because he hadn't won a bet after he bought it. Word was that his bookie was in the trunk at the time.

"So you'll do this for me. You'll do it and things'll change. If they don't . . . well, we'll do something else."

It was the something else that bothered me.

3

He'd arranged a room on the 18th floor. It wasn't a suite but it would do nicely: fully stocked bar, a bathtub long enough for laps, circular bed the size of a U.F.O., and mirrors strategically placed. The only negative was the color scheme, which was white, gold, and glitz.

I had stayed at the Grand once, before the Nugget sold out to Bally's. Nothing much had changed. The few high rollers were still being treated like royalty, while the pensioners, who bused in every day and really filled the joint, were treated with stony indifference. There's a class structure in casinos that goes beyond snobbery. But what's pride compared to greed?

To satisfy my own avarice, I'd brought a thousand bucks to play with, shrinking the small nest egg I'd set aside for a new car.

By seven o'clock I had napped, showered and shaved. I was hungry and went down to Charlie's Steak House just off the lobby.

I would have liked some company but so far the only unattached women I'd seen weren't really unattached. They were stuck to money and the Johns who provided it. As a hopeless romantic, I hated to pay for love. But I was miles from home and the night looked long and lonely.

The woman waiting at the maitre d's station could have passed for a working girl. About a hundred an hour. She had rich auburn hair in a perm and what she had on was a black one-piece jump suit that gave true meaning to its name. She appeared agitated. Her face had a pink glow and I couldn't tell if she'd spent the afternoon on the beach or she was simply hot with aggravation.

She kept scanning her watch. Was she late? I couldn't imagine anyone standing her up. Suddenly the thought of paying for love held new appeal. I winked. She left.

I shrugged it off.

I finished dinner and hit the casino. The first slot was loaded with fruit—cherries, plums, and oranges. It had some black and silver bars and some scattered sevens, but catching three on a line was unlikely.

I was playing the machine for the same reason that brought me to Atlantic City: superstition. Once, a long time ago, I'd won a few grand in Vegas. The night had begun with a jackpot from a slot like this one. It created a pattern, but not this night, until.

On my tenth spin I hit the triple seven. A thousand dollars was paid to me in cash by a dour floor manager who acted like the payoff was a drain on his kid's tuition. But the machine had told me what I needed to know: this was my night!

Within an hour at the craps table I'd doubled my winnings and was hoping for a bigger score when, from across the table, someone said, "Keep it up."

I looked over and saw the femme from the restaurant.

How long she'd been there I didn't know. But her rack was loaded with chips and from the smile on her face I knew she was winning.

"Keep it up," she said again as I shook the dice. "You're doing great."

The way to make money at craps is to roll as many numbers as you can before you seven out. I was on my fifth consecutive pass and my luck seemed uncanny. Eights and sixes, sixes and eights. The Texans loved it and they loved me for making them winners.

My current number was four—Little Joe—a bitch to make and a bane to shooters. She yelled, "Hard four!" and tossed a twenty-five dollar chip at the croupier.

I liked her confidence so I followed suit. "C'mon, baby, double deuce!"

The cheers rang out before the croup had called it. "Four," he honked. "Hard four."

When finally I did lose the dice I was up five large. Enough for one night, I thought.

Apparently my new friend agreed. "Good idea," she called to me as I gathered my chips. "Let's find the bank and break it."

She had the body of a showgirl and a name to match. "I'm Roxanne Ducharme," she said, after we'd cashed in and had stuffed our bags and pockets with loot.

"Frankie Fontana," I said.

We shook hands but she held on a bit too long to be casual. She tapped her purse. "Seven grand. That'll cure what hurts."

"Ain't that the truth?" I said. "What do you say, Roxanne? Should we celebrate?"

She hesitated a moment, a very brief moment, pursed her lips and said, "What do you have in mind?"

·   ·   ·

21

Our rooms were on the same floor. We chose mine; it was closer. Roxanne had the fever and I wasn't about to cool it off with any practical suggestions, like securing our money. She was willing to chance it, so was I.

But affairs, no matter how frivolous, often lead to complications. Gone were the days when I tended bar and all I had to lose was a failing marriage. Now it was different. I was married to my business and the risks, oddly, were greater.

What Roxanne could do with ice. Either Roxanne Ducharme was a pro, or she was doing a damn good imitation. My estranged wife was the best lover I'd ever had. But it was only sporadic. The moon had to be in conjunction with Jupiter for her. Not Roxanne.

We covered every inch of the bed, and every inch of our bodies. The mirrors helped the show-and-tell in those moments when I hadn't the slightest idea what she was doing or how she was doing it. It was the kind of sex that deserved strong words of endearment. So I waited for the pounding in my chest to subside, and said, "You gotta be kidding."

We were on our backs, looking at each other in the overhead mirror. Her skin was the color of honey and she had a slim waist, a flat stomach and a great set of wheels that led to the wildest patch of pubic hair I'd ever seen. It was dyed a garish red and trimmed to the shape of a heart.

I reached down and stroked it. She lay there, watching me in the mirror. "You like it?"

"Well," I said, "it answers one question."

"What's that?"

"What you do for a living. You work for a chocolate company, right? I mean that's one helluva Valentine."

She laughed for a moment, then gave me a kiss. "Speaking of Valentines, who gave you that one?" she said.

I pointed to the scar on my shoulder. "This? Compliments of Mrs. Fontana."

She reached down beside the bed where she'd discarded her clothes and purse. She fished out a cigarette, fired it up and tossed the purse back on the floor. The way she did it gave me cause for concern. After all, there was seven grand in there. It made me think of the former Mrs. F and the love she had for money. Given the choice between me and seven grand, there's no question which of the two she'd throw on the floor.

I frowned. Roxanne saw it and said, "What's the matter? Smoke bother you?"

"No," I said. "I was just thinking about my wife."

"Oh, no," she said. "Not another one. What is it with you married guys? Don't you ever stay home?"

"I would if there was someone there."

"Come on," she said. "You can do better than that."

She blew a jet of smoke from her nose. "Wanna know what I was up to tonight? I had a date with somebody's husband."

"And he stood you up," I said.

"Naturally. So what do I do? Pick up with another one." She sat up. "Well, it was nice knowing you, Frankie."

"Listen."

"Don't bother, I know every word."

"I'll bet you don't," I said.

She eyed me with the wariness of a true skeptic. "I'll stay if you come up with something I haven't heard before." She shrugged.

"My wife's away—in prison."

"Well," she said. "Yeah. That's one I haven't heard."

I reached over and massaged the back of her neck. Her eyes closed and she moaned softly.

4

Roxanne was face down on a towel, the top of her suit un-hooked, her legs and back slick with lotion. I'd wanted to stay in the room and play, but she had a tan to work on. So there I was on a beach chair, squinting up at a blinding sun, squirming uncom-fortably in the suit she'd bought me. She had picked it up in the gift shop while I was asleep. It was the size of a loincloth.

There wasn't much more to Roxanne's suit, some strings and a few essential patches. Storage was a problem for her too, but it didn't seem to bother her.

I said, "I feel ridiculous in this thing."

She peered over at me. "I think it's cute."

"Yeah," I said. It was only eighty degrees but the sun made it feel like a hundred. "How long do we stay?"

"A few hours. Why? Don't you like the beach?"

"I'm not used to it." I gazed out at the pounding surf. "I'm a night person."

"You're telling me. I haven't been this sore since my last karate lesson."

"Karate, eh? I wondered where you learned those moves."

"I've got a million of them," she said.

"That's what I'm afraid of. You know, you still haven't told me about yourself."

She lifted herself onto her elbows, flicked her shades and looked in my direction. "I thought we agreed, Frankie. Two days of fun and a wake-up."

"I'm not asking you to marry me, Roxanne. All I want is a little conversation. I'm bored, and this sun is frying my brain."

"Look," she said, "I already told you. I'm not a hooker. I've got a man who takes care of me. That's all you have to know."

"I saw the way he takes care of you," I said. "But hey, that's fine." I got up. "Enjoy the sun."

"Where you going?"

"Upstairs."

"You're pissed."

"Not really. I want to sleep and I'd rather do it in bed in an air conditioned room."

She squawked as I walked away. I ignored her because she was right. The only thing I needed to know about Miss Ducharme was that she'd been around the block more times than a Good Humor truck. Yet as I trudged across the hot sand toward the boardwalk, I had a feeling.

My room was cold and dark. I pulled the curtains, lowered the air and placed a call to my restaurant.

It was too early for Sally so I spoke to Harold, my day man. He assured me there'd been no shoot outs, that except for the blocked commode in the ladies' room, the place was still intact.

"I don't know what they do in there," Harold said. "But every time they flush, it's Mt. Saint Helen's."

"Call the plumber again," I said. "Tell him if it's not fixed by tomorrow I'll sic the Petrones on him. If that doesn't bring him then the boys are losing their touch."

After Harold, I spoke with the head chef who was having problems with an oven. Then one of the waitresses got on. Her kid had taken sick and she had to leave right away. Like I'd told Sally, it's not easy being rich.

I hung around for the rest of the day. At five o'clock the phone rang.

Roxanne.

"What are you doing?" she said.

"Just sitting around. I'm trying to figure out why I'm here."

"Still mad at me?"

"No, no. You were right."

I waited for her to reply but all I got was an awkward silence. "So how's the tan?" I said.

"Why don't you see for yourself? There's a whole night to go, you know."

"Where's your friend?"

"Home with his wife. So, what do you say? Want to try your luck again? We made a pretty good team last night."

"I always liked contact sports," I said.

We picked up where we'd left off in the casino. I insisted on playing the machines first. Roxanne knew about gamblers' quirks and went along with it. I wowed her with a three-bar jackpot at a hundred to one.

"We're unstoppable," I said, as the silver dollars clanked down the chute.

She rubbed her hands together, kissed me and said, "Come on, Lucky, let's rattle those bones."

She took my arm and we headed for the tables. Roxanne looked great. Her white mini-dress and copper skin drew venomous looks from women and comments from men. But she was mine and not afraid to show it.

"How about this one?" she said, stopping at one of the craps tables.

It was still too early for the heavy action. Most of the tables were quiet. The one she picked had four shooters, including a tall urban cowboy. He was shouting and carrying on like Bally's had built the place for his own personal pleasure. He was a Texan with a runaway mouth, and he reeked of oil and money.

He lit up when he saw Roxanne. Then he caught me moving in.

"Ya'll together?" he said.

I looked up at him. "Like Dale and Roy."

He gave me a look but said nothing. It was his turn to shoot and he waited while I bought a thousand in chips.

"Are you any good?" I asked.

"Just tra me," he drawled.

I dropped the whole pile on the pass line. "Go to it, Tex."

He smiled broadly. We were friends now, betting together.

"Ah do believe ah got me a pa'tner in crime," he announced. "Here we go, lil' lady. Blow awn these for ole Jamie Downs."

Roxanne blew daintily into his fist. "Go get 'em."

With one long finger he pushed the hat off his forehead. Then he drew back his arm, rattled the dice until they clicked like castinets, paused, and fired.

"Seven! Seven a natural," the croup intoned in a nasal voice.

"Kiss ma cute Texas ass!"

"Let it ride!" Roxanne urged.

He did and we rode with him.

I didn't know how much I was winning. Chips piled up faster than I could count. My heart pounded with every pass. I had the cold sweats and, for the first time in years, I craved a good cigar. Chips were flying and so was I.

Then someone tugged my arm. An unwelcome distraction that could only break the streak. Annoyed, I shrugged it away. It persisted.

"What?" I snapped. "What is it?"

"Hey!" Roxanne said, then whispered, "Take it easy."

It took a few seconds to come down. "How we doing?" I said.

"We're up twenty-five thousand. I think that's enough for now, Frankie. Don't you?"

For a second I wasn't sure I heard right. No one quits hot. But she gripped my arm and shook her head.

I smiled. "Is the fever that obvious?"

She nodded.

"Come on," I said. "Let's get a drink." I shook the Texan's hand, wished him luck, and walked away.

I'd no sooner left the table when I felt the tension lift, more with every step as we ambled across the casino floor.

The bar was in a corner, on a platform surrounded by a railing that separated the gamblers from the drinkers. It was more like a pit stop than a lounge, a place where losers pulled in and lamented, and winners rejoiced and refueled, before going back out again.

Roxanne wanted a table away from the bar, against the railing. "We can check the action and be admired at the same time," she said.

I understood. Roxanne liked to be looked at. She reminded me of the first Mrs. Fontana that way.

We ordered drinks and I watched Roxanne light a cigarette. Her eyes glistened in the flame. They were hazel with flecks of green. She was looking better by the minute and I had to warn myself to back off.

While I drank, Roxanne eyed me closely, her arms folded on the table, the purse under her hands. She'd fallen silent and I wasn't sure why.

"What's wrong?" I said.

"Nothing. Just trying to figure you out."

"What's to figure? Remember the deal? Fun and—"

"Yeah, I know." She patted her purse. "Do you have any idea how much we've got in here?"

"Seventeen dollars," I said, stealing a line from an old *Honeymooners* skit. "Including a postage stamp and an Indian head penny."

"Over thirty thousand, Frank. I've never had this much cash money in my life."

"You're just a poor kid from the ghetto," I said.

"Don't be like that." She pouted. "I'm trying to tell you something."

"What's that?"

She flushed the way women often do when they want you to think they're embarrassed. Roxanne wasn't the coy type, so I was wary. Whatever she wanted to tell me was apparently lodged between her head and her throat. She kept biting her lip, staring down at her cigarette like she was too flustered to look at me. I love it when the hard ones pull their little-girl routine. It's bullshit but it melts me right down. What can I say? Some guys never learn.

I took her hand, stroked it gently, smiled benignly, and waited.

When she did look at me, there was more dew in her eyes than Forest Lawn on a spring morning. "You're a nice guy, Frankie," she said.

I braced myself. Nice guy means shmuck and that's always trouble.

"The way you trust me with all this money," she went on. "I mean . . . I don't know. You don't even know me."

"Who's fault is that?"

"Yeah, I admit it. I made the rules and I have to play them out. I'm not used to men like you, that's all."

"I appreciate the thought, Roxanne."

"What about you?" she said. "Are you happy?"

I shrugged. "We won, didn't we?"

I couldn't tell if it was me or what. But her mood seemed to lift.

"Hello, Roxanne. How you doing?"

I looked up at a short, wiry guy with wispy hair and a beak that looked like someone had stepped on it. There was a forced smile under the nose, as if he knew something I didn't. I figured it pertained to Roxanne but that didn't help.

Roxanne played it casual. "For heaven's sake," she said. "Carmine. What are you doing here?"

"Same as you. How's it going? Had any luck?"

"Some," she said with a slight twinkle in those hazel-green eyes.

"Me, too," said Carmine. "Only mine's all bad. Okay if I sit?"

She looked to me for the okay.

I didn't like him or his smile. "He's *your* friend," I said.

She gave him the go ahead and he sat between us, facing out toward the casino floor.

"Name's Carmine Genovese," he said, sticking out his hand. "No relation."

"Fontana," I said with a slight frost.

His eyes shifted around. Then *he* shifted around, glancing from side to side as if checking for eavesdroppers. "Can I talk?"

"I don't know," I said. "Something wrong with your throat?"

"Come on," he said. "You know what I mean."

"Look," I said, "I want to be nice. But you're breaking the mood over here. You know what I mean?"

"Yeah," he said. He turned to Roxanne. "How do *you* feel about it, Rox?"

"The same," she said. "But I'm sentimental about old friends. So have a drink. Then leave."

"Sure. Sure thing, Rox. I was gonna put you onto something big. But if that's the way you feel . . ." He picked up the drink he'd brought with him. "I'll just finish this and get outta your hair. Too bad though. You could fall into a ton load'a shit if you'd listen to me."

I said, "Finish your drink."

"Your friend don't know me. He don't know I can smell action a mile away. Tell him. Tell him about this nose of mine."

"She doesn't have to," I said. "It's been busted a few times. And I can see why."

"Take it easy," Roxanne said. "All right, Carmine. You're dying to tell me about it. Go ahead."

"Don't know if I should. I mean, why help this creep? He's being damn rude, if you don't mind me saying it. But all right." He put down his drink and said, "You're gonna love this. Remember Alfie Betso?"

Roxanne grimaced. "Fat Alfie?"

"None other. Well, he's up on the twelfth floor. Got a sweet little game going. Five grand buy-in, table stakes and no horseshit. You know how bad Alfie plays. He's kinda hot right now but that's cause there ain't nobody up there knows a straight from a pair'a deuces. I figured you might wanna mosey up there and show 'em how to play. Whadaya say?"

"Sure," Roxanne said. "I'll walk in there and lift up my dress. That's the only way they'll let me play and you know it."

Carmine snickered. "I know that. But your friend can play. How about it, friend? You play poker?"

"In the schoolyard," I said. "For baseball cards and bottle caps."

Carmine looked grim. "You better tell this guy to stop fuckin' around, Rox. I'm trying to put you onto a score. It ain't right, the way he's treating me."

"If it's that easy," I said, "why don't *you* go up? What do you need us for?"

He snorted. "You're the one's had the luck. I been hittin' a rock all fucking day."

"So what's in this for you?" I said.

"You gotta know somebody to get you in. For five hundred I'll clear the way."

"Forget it," I said. "I don't like private games. Especially in this town. Too many sharks."

"You don't know Betso," he said. "Tell him, honey. Tell him how Danny D. took him for more than a hundred grand last year. Ever see Danny anymore?"

"No," she said curtly.

"But you remember how dumb Danny was. Your man here, he looks smart. Sure talks it. Shit, Rox, if Danny could clip a hundred off'a Betso, think what he could do? All you need's a little luck, for Chrissake."

"We'll think about it," she said.

"Suit yourself. But don't think too long. Time you get up there, somebody else'll clean him out."

"We'll think about it," she said again.

"I'll be at the bar. Make it quick. I'm down to my last sawbuck and I feel a run coming on. I won't say it's been a pleasure, Fontana. 'Cause it ain't."

Carmine sauntered away.

"Nice man," I said to Roxanne.

"Carmine's a leech," she said. "He lives in these joints. Sucks around the big money boys hoping for scraps. But he's right about that nose of his. Wherever there's action, that's where you'll find him."

"Who's Danny D.?"

"A mistake."

"And Betso?"

"A loser. Plays poker the way he eats. Every hand is too good to pass up. Danny told me about him. Called Betso the worst card player he ever saw. It's amazing when you think what he does for a living."

"What's that?"

"He's a shylock."

"I don't like shylocks," I said.

"Then you'll hate Betso. Everybody does. He's an obnoxious son of a bitch. That's why it's so much fun to beat him at his own game."

"Wait a minute," I said. "Are you saying we ought to go up there?"

"Maybe."

"I wasn't kidding about the schoolyard, Roxanne."

"Baseball cards and bottle caps? Come on, Frankie. You're too sharp with the dice to be a novice. You've played poker before."

"Sure," I said. "One and two. Never table stakes. One big bump and I'm out of there."

"You won't have to see the raise. Play it cautious. If you don't have the hand, you can always fold. Besides, what do we have to lose? Five thousand? We're still up thirty, counting last night."

"Sure," I said, "provided Carmine isn't pulling a fast one. How do I know it's not a set up? Forget about the game for a minute. What if he's got some friends in that room? We walk in, they grab our money and leave us with bloody scalps. I mean, how do I know?"

"You don't," she said.

"Thank you."

"Unless," she added quickly, "you believe what I say."

"Why should I?"

"Hey," she said. "I've been straight with you, Frankie, so don't insult me. I'm telling you, Carmine is harmless. He's in this for the five hundred. To him that's big bucks."

"All right," I said. "Forget Carmine for a minute. Tell me about Betso."

She sighed. "I already did."

"Yeah, I know. He's a shylock with bad luck. Nice, but it doesn't compute. Shys are like bookies. They thrive on everyone else's bad luck. That's why they can do what they do."

"Maybe you're right," she said. "Maybe Betso is lucky. But not with cards. I tell you, we can parlay five grand into more money than we'll ever see again."

"I don't know," I said.

But Roxanne knew enough for both of us. At least it seemed that way. Her eyes had the familiar sparkle. She was staring at me but all she could see was an easy score.

She squinted out from under her long lashes, batted them a few times and said, "I'll bet there's two to three hundred thousand in that game, Frankie. I can buy a new start with that kind of money. Tell them all to kiss my ass."

"Including your married friend?"

"Him first," she said. "Oh, would I love that."

"I'd love it, too."

"So what do you say?"

"Guess I'm a sucker for the downtrodden."

5

The room on the twelfth floor resembled a proving grounds for chemical warfare. There was so much smoke and foul air I could barely see the cards.

Carmine had gotten us in but not before we had passed muster with Fat Alfie Betso. He had his own superstitions and women were high on his list. He didn't want them around while he played.

"You can stay," he told me in a whiskey voice. "But the fluff's gotta go."

"She's my banker," I said. "If she goes, so do I."

There were five players and a dealer sitting around an over-sized table, one of those green felt jobs with slots and trenches for drinks and chips. Betso's fat belly overhung the trench in front of him. Under all that flesh I could see his chips. He was well ahead, and seemed resolved to keep it that way.

It was one of the players who convinced him. A likeable character named Willie. "Come on, Alfie," he said, "let her stay. If we're gonna lose, at least give us a pretty face to look at. Besides, her boyfriend looks like fresh meat."

Betso hesitated, but not for long. His disdain for women was no match for his appetite. The sight of fresh meat had him salivating.

"All right," he said. "But she keeps outta sight." He looked over at Roxanne. "Ain't I seen you somewhere?"

"I doubt it," she said. "I'm sure you'd remember."

"Yeah," he said. "One thing I don't forget is a Jonah."

He aimed a pudgy finger at the couch behind him. "Sit," he told her. "Keep your yap shut. And don't make with the eyes either. I see you makin' eyes at your boy and you're both out on your ass."

I glared at Betso, at his three chins and fat lips. I was showing him my tough-guy look, but I wasn't scaring anyone. For an easy mark, Fat Alfie looked damn hard to take.

The dealer's name was Jake, a gloomy, taciturn man of about forty who called the cards like an intensive care patient on life support. I let a few rounds pass, sacrificing one or two pots I thought I could win. It was part of the reconnoiter, a necessary investment for the big payoff.

Poker is the only game I know where you can tell by the first few hands how the cards are going to run. I liked what I was seeing but it takes more than good cards to win at poker. It's knowing the competition that does it.

It didn't take long to size up this bunch. Poker players are not aware of their own habits. But they all have them and if you're patient and play it cautious, they're there to spot.

I could see right away why Carmine had labeled Betso a loser. He was a chaser, the kind of player who wouldn't fold his hand no matter what he held. To Betso the odds never seemed to matter, any draw was possible. Especially when the pot was fat.

The game was five card stud. The stakes were one hundred dollars, double on a pair. Raising, however, was limited only by the amount of chips a player had in his trench.

The times I folded, I noticed Jake giving me the fish eye. But he didn't speak or show emotion. I wasn't surprised. I'd never known a dealer who wasn't dead from the neck up.

I was seated mid-table, across from him. Willie and Betso were on my right, the other players to my left. Betso drew a queen, Willie an ace. I got a king and so did the guy next to me. The king I got matched the one I had in the hole.

"One hundred," Willie said.

I called and the rest dropped out. Except for Betso.

"Make it five," he said.

I wasn't worried about him. The most he could have were a pair of queens. Willie was the key. If he'd paired his ace he would bump. But he only called.

"Whadaya say, Lover?" Betso said. He'd been calling me Lover from the time I sat down. Each time he did, Roxanne would burn the back of his neck with a hot glare. But he couldn't see it and that was fine with me.

"Five more," I said.

I didn't think he'd be crazy enough to kick me back. But he was angered by my raise and, like every chaser, he wouldn't give in.

"Once more," he said.

Willie folded his ace and Betso and I were left head to head.

I had him beat but I couldn't show it. He wanted me out of the game and for these stakes, it wouldn't be hard to accomplish. I had to play him along, make him think he had me. It was a strategy I'd stay with until I was rich enough to scare him off.

"Call," I said.

"Coming out," Jake droned. "King to the queen. Five to the king. King-queen bets."

I couldn't have asked for a better draw. It put Betso in the lead and that meant he couldn't raise. It stayed that way until the last card, neither of us improving our hand. Betso was still high with the king-queen. But the case king was out so there was no way to beat me.

In games like this you're allowed to double the bet on the last card. "Two hundred," Betso said.

"Make it a thousand," I said.

One thing I love about fat guys is their blood pressure. When they're pissed they get red in the face. Betso's grim visage took on the scarlet hue of Roxanne's hair. He sputtered and rolled around in his chair like a blimp in a high gale.

"You mother fucker!" he said. "You sandbagged. You fuckin' sandbagged." He reached over and spread my chips like he owned them. "How much you got there?"

I was ripping mad over the way he was treating my money. But he was madder than me and that cooled me off real fast.

"I don't know," I said. "You tell me."

"Put it up. Whatever it is, put it up. I'm raisin' what you got."

I was doing my riverboat gambler imitation, fingering my chips, counting them slowly and casually. "What I got is thirty-four hundred," I said.

"Put it in."

I scooped out my chips and tossed them on the table.

"All right," Betso said, turning over his cards. "I got queens. You beat queens?"

Willie laughed. "Of course he beats 'em. What the hell you think he's playin' for?"

39

I showed my kings.

"Kings wired," Betso said in disbelief. "You gutless bastard! Why didn't you raise before?"

"If you recall," I said, "I raised on the first card."

"*One* raise? Big fuckin' deal. You got kings wired you're supposed to bet 'em. Why didn't you raise?"

I raked in the money. "Greed blinds me," I said. "Always has."

It went like that for the rest of the night. The wilder Betso got, the more he chased and the more he lost. Mostly to me. The truth is, if I see a hundred years I'll never see another run like that one. No matter what anyone pulled, it was never enough to beat me. By one a.m. I was up over two hundred thousand dollars. I had cleaned out everyone except Willie and Betso. But Willie was on the brink and I knocked him out with an ace high flush.

Willie sighed. "That's it for me, ladies and germs. Tapsville." He got to his feet and began rubbing my back. "I'll take some of the shit you got on you for tomorrow," he said. "Take any help you can get, that's my motto."

Betso was livid. Most of my winnings had belonged to him before I got there. In the span of three hours I had turned his dream night upside down.

"It's that cunt!" he bellowed. "*She* did it."

Alfie Betso was a big man with a big mouth. His mouth didn't scare me and I never knew a fat man who could fight. So I stiffened up, looked him in the eye and said, "You better watch your mouth, fat man."

Willie dropped heavily into his chair as if he'd caught a bullet in the head. Even Jake blanched.

Meanwhile, Betso was eyeing me as though I'd just materialized out of cigarette smoke. He blinked several times, cocked his oversized head, furrowed his brow and peered at me through the blue-white haze. When he did finally speak it came out in an ominous whisper.

"What did you say?"

It struck me suddenly that all I knew about Fat Alfie Betso was that he shylocked. That should have been enough. I knew a lot of shys, and every one of them had the knack of being mean and nasty. Especially when it came to getting back their money.

"I'm waiting," he said.

It took Willie to bail me out. He slapped me on the back, forced a laugh and said, "He didn't mean it, Alfie. He's in love, that's all. Anybody called my girl a cunt, I'd do the same thing."

Betso looked at him. He was grinning at Willie like he didn't believe him for a second. I looked at Willie and didn't believe him either.

It was during this brief exchange that Roxanne drifted over. She'd pulled in behind me and was holding my shoulder as if she expected me to start throwing punches and meant to stop me. It was a sweet but unnecessary gesture.

"Let's go, Frankie," Roxanne said, breaking the silence.

I knew what Betso was going to say: "He ain't going nowhere. You're the one's going. Take your choice, the window or the door. Makes no fucking difference to me."

"You better go," I told her.

"That's right. Kiss him good-bye. Get lost."

"Is that the way it is?" she said to Betso. "You keep playing until you win back your money?" She turned to Willie. "What is this, lendsies? You get *your* money back, too?"

Lowering his head, Willie said, "She's right, Alfie."

Bless you Willie, I thought.

"Stay outta this," Betso said. "You're tapped anyway. I'm not. I got fifty g's in front of me. We play until it's gone. Or he's gone."

I looked at Jake. "Is that the rule?"

41

Betso snapped, "What the fuck you askin' *him* for? I'm the one's got the bread. He deals. And he better do a better job or he ain't gonna be dealin' no more. Not ever."

"All right," I said, "On one condition."

"Condition?" Betso said. "The only *condition* you're gonna be in is horizontal. You believe this guy, Willie? Takes my money and he wants conditions."

"He didn't take it, Alfie. He won it."

"Fair and square," I said.

"I gotcha, fair and square," Betso said. "Now do we play? Or do I rip your fuckin' heart out?"

"Deal them, Jake," I said without pause or conditions.

"Willie, say good night," Betso snorted, "and take the bitch with you."

Roxanne gave me a kiss. "See you later," she whispered. "Be careful."

"Yeah," Betso said. "Be real careful."

It took two more hours to blitz Mr. Betso. My cards weren't as good as before the blow up, but they were good enough. The outcome was never in doubt. As they say on the street, a lock!

My only problem was getting out of there in one piece. Willie wasn't around to referee and Jake was so intimidated that I was sure he'd dig my grave if Betso ordered him to.

About all I could do was cozy up to Fat Alfie Betso. Or try. I was sure he had muscle behind him. Shys always have goons on their payroll. Gives them credibility. I didn't know where the goons were penned up and I sure as hell didn't care to find out. I'd won three hundred and twenty-five thousand dollars.

"That's a lota money," Betso said, watching as I filled every pocket with bills. He was still sitting there, baggy eyed and slack jawed. Now that it was over, he seemed a lot calmer. Maybe too calm.

"One of those nights," I said. "You know how it is. Look, I'm sorry about what I said. I was outta line."

"Somebody was outta line. I ain't sure who. That was some kind'a run you had tonight. Unreal, you know?"

"That's the way it is with cards."

"Yeah," Betso said, "the way it is."

Jake was just coming out of the bathroom. I could tell he was nervous. He kept rubbing his eyes, looking at everything but us.

"It's a good thing Jake was dealing," Betso said. "We go back a long way, Jake and me. Ain't that right?"

"A long way." Jake looked like an out patient with sudden symptoms. "Okay to leave now?"

"If I didn't know better," Betso said, ignoring him, "I'd swear those cards were comin' off the bottom."

Jake's face turned to paste. The only blood he had left was in his eyes. He squinted at Betso and offered a pained smile. "Holy shit, Bets. You think I'd . . . I mean . . . holy shit . . . I'd never . . ."

Jake had to be a dealer. He couldn't talk well enough to play.

"Relax," Betso said. "If you were cheating I'd know. Besides, you have no reason. You never set eyes on this guy before tonight. That's true, ain't it, Jake?"

"Never!" Jake said. "Swear to God. I never . . . we don't . . . I mean . . ."

"Jake. Get outta here."

Jake was in such a rush that he scooted by me, missing the tip I was holding out for him. He was scared shitless. Why else pass up a thousand bucks?

I felt better with Jake gone. I didn't trust Betso but he seemed calm enough, and so far, at least, there was no sign of a weapon.

"Your name's Fontana, eh?"

"Yeah."

"Where you from, Fontana?"

If Betso wanted to fish it was all right with me. I just wouldn't bait his hook. "Ohio," I said.

"You're shittin' me."

"Born and raised," I said.

"You don't act like Ohio. You're more New York. Wouldn't lie to me, would you? I don't like liars."

"No lie," I said. "What about you?"

"All around. Mostly Jersey. Of course you wouldn't know that. From Ohio and all."

"Is Betso a big name in New Jersey?"

"Big enough. But I got friends in New York, too. Think I'll nose around. Make sure you ain't lying about this Ohio shit."

"All right," I said. "Let's cut the crap. I was born in Ohio, I live in Queens. You can find me easy enough. The question is, why? I mean if you plan on killing me for this money, whip out your piece and take it back right now. I'm no hero. I like money, but it's not worth dying for."

"I'm glad to hear that," he said. "What about your lady friend? You speak for her, too?"

"*I* won the money, not her. You got a problem, bring it to me."

"And you said you weren't a hero. See what I mean about fluff? They're Jonahs. All right, look. I'm gonna check you out. If you're straight, you got no problem. I'll figure you're just some asshole with more luck than I ever seen. But if this was some kind a scam . . . Well, you figure it out."

44

6

"My God," she said when I walked in. "I was so worried."

She looked it but I wasn't convinced. I had questions for Roxanne, questions I should have asked before getting involved in that game.

"Worried about what?" I said. "Me? Or the money?"

She looked hurt. "What do you mean?"

"You know damn well what I mean. You've got some explaining to do. And it better be straight shit, Roxanne. Or so help me, whatever I won from Betso will go right back."

"What are you saying? Are you crazy? You can't just give it back. He'll know something's wrong!"

"Then it *was* a scam. Carmine's the hook and Jake's the mechanic. All you needed was a shmuck like me. A guy dumb enough to think with his dick. Cute, Rox, real cute."

"No," she said. "I swear. I don't know Jake from Adam. Never saw him before tonight. You gotta believe me, Frankie."

"Sure I gotta believe you. So give me something to believe. I like you, Roxanne. But not enough to take you to heaven. Which is where we're going if you've lied to me. Don't look so shocked. People get killed for money. But I don't have to tell you that, do I?"

I placed my hands on her shoulders and sat her on the couch. "Tell me all you know about Betso. Just remember this, I know a few guys back home. If Betso's as big as I think, they'll know all about him."

"I told you," she said. "He's a loan shark."

"Not enough."

"He works out of Jersey City."

"A lotta shys work Jersey City," I said. "Is he protected?"

"What do you mean?"

"Do they protect him? Is he connected?"

"What do I know about that?" she said. "All I know is what my boyfriend, Danny, told me—that he's a fat slob and a born loser."

"He's fat and he can't play cards. But loser? He's too cocky to be a loser."

"What do you want me to say?" she stammered.

"Start with your boyfriend. How does he know Betso."

"Same as you. Through Carmine. Look, we're wasting time. Let's just take the money and get out of here. How much did you win?"

"Too much," I said. "It doesn't ring true. I mean I've been hot before, Roxanne, but never like this. Betso's suspicious. He's got a right to be. So am I, if you want the truth."

She got to her feet. "That's the craziest thing I ever heard. I saw the game, I listened. You beat him because you were better than he was. And luckier. Jesus, Frank, I know guys who'd give their eye teeth for the luck you had tonight. Isn't that what you wanted? What you've waited for all your life?"

"Speak for yourself," I said. "I was satisfied with what we had. Thirty grand, divided two ways."

"I don't believe this," she said. "You'd settle for dimes when you could have dollars? I thought you were sharper. I really did."

"So did I," I said. I shook my head. "I must be getting punchy. I swear I've been through this before. 'Deja vu all over again.'"

We fell silent. How do you get the truth from a woman who's blinded by dollar signs? About all I could do was stick close to Roxanne until I checked Betso out for myself.

I knew a few people who could help me, but if this *was* a scam and Betso got to them before I did, it wouldn't matter who I knew or what I said.

Roxanne had moved to the bar. She was mixing a drink and looked annoyed, her pink cheeks pinker than before.

"Never mind that," I said. "We're leaving."

"Thank God," she said. She left the drink and started for the door. "I'll go pack. Pick you up in fifteen minutes."

"You'll wait," I said. "Until this is over you're on a short leash tied to my wrist."

"You still don't trust me."

"Think of it as love," I said. "I can't stand being apart."

My luggage consisted of one suit bag and two blue gym bags with the New York Giants logo on them. After packing my shirts, jacket and slacks in the suit bag, I stuffed my toiletries, soiled shirts and underwear into one of the gym bags. The other bag held the money: three hundred and fifty thousand ever lovin' dollars.

As I counted the cash Roxanne's eyes glazed over and grew dark with visions. Fantasies fulfilled. It was a look I had seen too many times before, in my ex-wife's eyes. Only this time I understood what it meant.

I covered the money with dirty socks. "All set," I said. "Let's get your stuff and get out of here. I'm taking you with me to New York."

I figured she'd have plenty to say about that idea, but she took it calmly and without surprise. It was almost enough to convince me she'd been straight about all this. God knows it's what I wanted.

"What happens in New York?" she said.

"I nose around. If you haven't lied, we split the money. After that you can do what you want, go your merry way."

"What about us? I thought maybe you and I . . . you know."

"Yeah, I know. You want to get a villa in the Bahamas, live happily ever after on sunshine and love."

"Is that so terrible?"

"Not to me," I said. "But I doubt Mr. Betso would agree."

That Johnny Scarlo should pick up the tab for all this was downright laughable. But that was our deal and I accepted his comp with the grace of a good winner, wondering, as we checked out, what his reaction would be when I laid this one out for him. I prayed his luck had changed in my absence. Certainly mine had. I just didn't yet know how.

"Isn't that Carmine by the door?" I said as we were leaving the hotel.

Roxanne squinted toward the exit. "That leech," she said. "He got the word. He knows we won and he wants his payoff."

"He's about to get it," I said. "Dummy up. I'll do the talking."

Carmine was leaning against the glass wall alongside the door. "Whadaya know about that," he said as we approached. "Here I am, thinking about you guys, and what happens? Must be my lucky day." He stuck out his hand. "Good to see you, my man."

"Go wipe your ass," I said.

"Hey! That's no way to treat a meal ticket. I scored for you, pal. Least you can be is polite. Show some thanks, you know?"

"You mean money," I said.

"What a guy," he said to Roxanne. "Sharp as a fuckin' tack."

"All right," I said. "I'm going to ask you one question. Give me the right answer, Carmine. Or you're back on the bread line."

He raised his face and looked down at me from over that crooked nose of his. "Shoot," he said, all smiles, confident.

"Betso," I said. "Is he connected?"

"Yeah," he said. "To his fat ass. Whadaya mean connected? Everybody's connected in this town. Shit, even I'm connected. I got friends on the Shore."

"The only friends you got on the shore are crabs."

He laughed. "Yeah, that too. Little fuckers keep me awake at night. You ain't gonna sleep too good yourself, I think. Fat Alfie's pretty pissed right now. Thinks you cheated him. But he's an asshole. Blames everybody else when he loses. Which is always." He laughed harder. "Don't sweat it, Fontana. You beat him fair and when he finds out, you'll be okay. So how about it? A little smear for your friend, Carmine?"

"I'd like to smear you across this lobby," I said. "What you told me sucks. It's not worth a nickel. Now get out of my way."

I pushed him aside with both of my gym bags. A dumb move. He grabbed the nearest bag and tried to yank it away. "Is the money in here? This where you put it?"

"Let go of that!" Roxanne said. She saw what Carmine was trying to do. She karate kicked him in the shins. "Let it go, you jerk!"

Carmine was yelping, clutching his leg and hopping around on one foot. "You bitch!" he hollered. "Two timin' bitch!"

The one thing I didn't need was attention. Roxanne was

hopping mad and Carmine was hopping, period. He kept shouting obscenities and people were staring.

"Let's go," I said, shoving Roxanne out the door.

She was still muttering when the attendant brought out my car. I looked back; Carmine was beating a gimpy retreat past the reception desk. I tossed my clothes and the gym bag I was holding into the small trunk of my Buick Skyhawk.

"Give it over," I said, meaning the bag Roxanne held tightly against her breast.

"Let me hold it," she said. "I wanna hold it."

Having fought to defend it, it seemed only right. I nodded. "Get in."

She placed the bag between her feet, buckled up and settled back for what I hoped would be a quiet, uneventful drive. Sure. No one followed us out of the hotel driveway and I exhaled and tried to ease up.

"Not much traffic," Roxanne said as we entered the Garden State Parkway.

"Weekday," I said.

"We going to your place?"

"Maybe."

She reached down and squeezed the bag. "I feel like a Brink's guard." She said it lightly. "Okay if I smoke?"

"No."

"You planning to grunt like this all the way to New York?"

I looked at her and said nothing.

She was wearing white summer slacks and a black sleeveless jersey tucked at the waist by a wide belt, which she fussed with.

"You're mad at me again," she said. "All right, let's hear it."

"You did hear it," I said. "From Carmine."

She looked at me quizzically. "So what does that mean?" she said. "It's just a name he called me."

"You knew about that poker game, didn't you? That's why Carmine was looking for us. You paid him to lure me into it. What'd you do, promise him more if we won?"

She turned her face toward the window and gazed out at the bleak Jersey countryside. A long moment passed before she spoke.

"It's true," she said.

"Look at me," I said. "I wanna see your eyes."

She turned to me slowly. I expected tears and there they were. Women always cry when they've lied. It's so predictable it's scary.

"Why didn't you tell me outright what you had in mind?" I said. "Why bring Carmine into it?"

"Mistake," she said.

"What about Jake? Was he dealing straight?"

"Why wouldn't he?" she said. But her eyes began spilling over and I had some serious doubts.

"Let me tell you something, Roxanne. If that game was crooked, then both of us are in deep shit. Even if Betso isn't connected, he's bound to have shakers on his payroll. He'll send them. And believe me, when they catch us, that money will be the last thing you'll worry about."

She clammed up. I didn't press it. We both needed time to ponder what might well be a future measured in days, if not hours. I had meant to shake her up and so far it was working, on me.

Seven years ago I'd turned in my adding machine and number two Venus pencils, forsaking a safe, predictable career as an accountant. I was bored, and life in the fast lane was like a siren's call, the Manifest Destiny of American barhoppers. But old habits die hard, I guess. I had three hundred, fifty thousand dollars within arm's reach, a gorgeous female at my side, and all I could think of were debits and credits, balance sheets, profit and loss statements: the staid business of recording other people's assets.

I should have been thinking about the road.

"Look out!" Roxanne called.

Startled, I turned toward her.

"Next to you! He's gonna hit us!"

I hadn't see him, he was in the blind spot between the side and rearview mirrors. It took a second to pick him up and by then he was right alongside. Except it wasn't a he, it was they. Four men. Two in back, two in the front.

They swerved right, clipped my door and pulled back quickly. My little Hawk fishtailed but I straightened her out and kept her going.

"They're crazy!" Roxanne screamed.

"Never mind that. Tell me what they're doing."

"Whadaya mean? They're trying to kill us is what they're doing!"

I checked the side mirror but all I saw was the heavy grillwork of a big motor machine. A Lincoln, I think. Or a Sherman tank. Not that it mattered. My car was a golf cart by comparison, four lousy cylinders and one of those on the fritz.

I tried to gun it but speed and power were all on their side. I couldn't out run them or knock them down.

"Here they come again," Roxanne said, grunting as she fought the constraints of her seatbelt.

"Stay put," I told her.

"They're Betso's men, aren't they? My God, what do we do?"

"Hold on!"

I slammed the brake and cut right, skidding off the road onto the soft shoulder. They tried to stop but it was too late.

By the time they pulled over, I was stopped a good fifty yards behind them, sitting in a dust cloud that had settled over us like an isolated patch of fog.

"What the hell are you doing?" Roxanne shouted.

"Waiting for help," I said.

She craned her neck in every direction. "There's no one in sight, for Christ's sake."

"Cool it," I said.

But she was right. It was five-thirty in the morning and the parkway resembled a scene from a sci-fi movie. One of those flicks where the world's been decimated by nuclear fallout and all that's left in New Jersey are six people, four of whom are mutant killers.

Meanwhile, the guys in the Lincoln were eyeing us through the windows like they had nothing to kill but time. I guess they knew we weren't going anywhere. The Lincoln angled its nose out toward the road and waited. If only help would appear, someone or something to run interference for us. Anything would do. A bus, a truck, even a Hell's Angel on a Harley.

"Look!" Roxanne said. "They're fighting with each other."

"You wish," I said, but as I squinted out through the settling dust I could see the two guys in the back seat. They were fighting, all right. At least one of them was. The other guy was holding up his arms, fending off the blows. I couldn't figure it out until the guy taking the abuse was hauled up by his collar and had his face slammed against the window.

I looked at Roxanne.

"That's Jake," she said.

"No shit. Still wanna tell me that game wasn't fixed, Miss Ducharme?"

She lowered her face and covered it with her hands. "Not now, Frankie. Please, not now."

I was about to tell her that it was now or never, when, from the rear mirror, I spotted a shiny hunk of metal rising up over a knoll about a half mile away. "Someone's coming," I said.

She dropped her hands and turned around. "What are you going to do?"

"When he passes, we follow. I'll stay right on his ass. They won't try anything with a witness. All we have to do is stay close to him."

She gazed ahead at the big Lincoln, its engine purring, the driver hunched over the wheel like a kamikaze pilot chained to his joy stick. Jake was still there, looking forlorn as hell. But we had our own problems and little time to work them out.

"What if they have guns?" Roxanne said.

"I'm sure they do."

"It's not just us anymore, Frankie."

"Then get out and hand over the money," I said. "If you're lucky they'll let you live long enough for them to count it. Here he comes."

I headed straight for the Lincoln. The fifty yards would give me the running start I needed to tuck in behind my blocker, who was coming on steady and fast. But the bad guys weren't stupid. They knew what I was doing and they were ready for it. They pulled out as the new guy went by me. He hit his brakes at the precise moment I slipped in behind him.

Roxanne screamed. I would have screamed, too, if I wasn't praying. I had visions of a three car smack up and a fiery death, while Betso's cash sailed and fluttered above the wreckage like so many feathers from a shot duck.

But the guy ahead of us must have trained in Indianapolis. He hooked a quick left and then right and did it all in one smooth motion. Caught in his draft, I swooped in after him, passing three startled goons and one slightly damaged dealer.

What we had now was a snappy little motorcade comprised of Mario Andretti, us in the middle, and one pissed-off caboose.

7

When I bought my car, the seller called it "reliable transportation." By that he meant that it started and stopped when it was supposed to. Until today I hadn't cared much about the in between, she'd always been fine from zero to forty. Eighty was another matter.

"Do something, Frankie. We're losing him."

"What's that guy driving?" I said as we shuddered and shook and the lead car began pulling away.

"It's a Nissan," Roxanne said. "Two-eighty ZX."

"What the hell does that mean?"

"It means he's faster than us."

"There's gotta be somebody else on this fucking road. What's going on behind us?"

She turned and peered over the front seat. "They're dropping back. No . . . wait . . . they're coming on. My God," she screamed, "they're gonna ram us!"

I checked the mirror. They were so close I could see their faces, one smiling, the other grim and determined. They banged us once. We lurched forward. They hit us again. Only this time they didn't back off, they stayed on us, pushing us faster and faster.

The speedometer bounced off eighty and we bounced along with it. I was giving gas but it wasn't our power moving us. It was a big ass Lincoln with more r.p.m's than a frigging Concorde.

"That's it," Roxanne cried out. "Give it up. Pull over!"

"How?" I said. "I can't stop. If I turn the wheel they'll flip us over."

"I'll stop them," she said.

She undid the belt, turned, kneeled in her seat and began waving frantically.

"It's no use," I said.

"No, look. They're pulling back."

They slowed down and I followed suit. Something was burning under the hood but so far we hadn't blown anything. I still had power and for a second I considered jumping the divider.

But Roxanne had her own plan, and getting killed in a burning car crash wasn't part of it.

"Stop the car," she said. "We're going to fight them."

I looked at her like she was nuts. "Are you nuts?" I said.

"Shut up," she replied. "I'll take one out right away. That leaves one each. We can do it."

As we debated the pros and cons of fisticuffs, the boys in the Lincoln settled the matter. They blew their horn and, when I caught them in the mirror, the guy riding shotgun was waving one at us. A sawed off job with twin barrels.

There isn't a man alive who hasn't envisioned his own death,

where it will be and how it will happen. I've pondered hundreds
of possibilities in my time, but getting blown away on the Garden
State Parkway was one that never occurred to me. Karate my ass!

I pulled into the emergency lane, stopped the car on the
shoulder and killed the motor. The pings and groans of the
Hawk's mini-engine, as it cooled, sounded like a frightened
chorus. The Nissan was long gone. The Lincoln pulled up and
parked behind us. Some light traffic was coming but it was too
late to help. Unless.

"Do what I do," I told Roxanne.

"I'm not running!"

"I know. Come on."

I stepped out and away from the car, my hands raised, and
dropped to my knees. "Don't shoot!" I hollered. "Don't shoot!"

It wasn't hard to act scared. I was. Scared and desperate
enough to bet against public apathy. Only a cold and callous son
of a bitch would pass up two people on their knees praying for
help.

The first car zipped by without a look. The second, a station
wagon with a family of kids, slowed a bit, then took off, pointing
when Roxanne fell to her knees beside me.

"All right you two assholes. Get up!"

He had the shotgun. But it was aimed at the ground, along his
side, so no one would see it. I could have told him not to bother,
these citizens wouldn't stop if he splattered our brains all over the
parkway.

"Around this side," he said, nodding his head away from the
road. Behind him in the distance oil refineries fired the dawn sky
with gas flames. The smell was like Godzilla breaking wind.

The Lincoln inched closer but no one else got out. So far it was
just him against us. Him and the shotgun.

He looked like one of those guys you see wielding oversized

hammers in body-fender shops. Six feet tall, cruddy jeans, worn out boots and a tight fitting T-shirt that stretched across his belly and pumped out his biceps like a pair of helium balloons. He had hairy arms and grimy fingers, one of which gripped the trigger while another was held out in front of him for stage direction.

He pointed to the door of my Buick. "If it's in there, get it out."

"Get what out?" Roxanne said.

He grinned at me through a set of cracked teeth. "What did ya do," he said, "fuck her brains out? Come on, bitch, you know what I mean."

"You work for Betso?" I said.

"No," he said, grinning. "Robin Hood. We rob from the rich to give to the poor. Now come on. You got a bag full 'a money in there. Get it out and hand it over."

As though it made a difference, I said, "What happens to us?"

"You ain't too bright yourself," he said.

"Maybe you're right," I said. "So if you're going to kill us, do it now."

He winced and gave Roxanne the eye like he wanted confirmation. Of course she had no idea what I had in mind, which made us even. I didn't know what she was scheming either, until she said, "Speak for yourself. I don't plan to get myself killed for a few lousy dollars."

How quickly they forget, I thought.

"Listen," she told the gunman. "This whole thing was his idea. I've got nothing to do with it. The money's right in the car. Take it. Him, too, for all I care."

He shook his head and offered me a look of mutual understanding, like a man who's been had by women a few times in his life. A different time and place, and who knows, we might have commiserated over a few beers.

"Sorry, pal," he said. "But you fucked up and that's that. All right, Princess, get the money."

She opened the door, fished the bag and held it out to him. "It's all here," she said. "Every dollar."

"Lemme have it," he said.

"Certainly," Roxanne said.

What followed was like a scene from a movie: *Bruce Lee Meets The Three Stooges*. Lemme have it, Moe says, pointing to a lemon meringue pie. Soint'ly, replies Curly.

Except the pie was a bag of money and it didn't hit Moe's face but his stomach. Moe caught it and Roxanne Ducharme caught him, square in the chest with the tip of her pointed heel.

For a while it was all fun and games: heavy slapstick, with me doing the slapping and Moe getting the stick. It wasn't too hard to work him over. He was face down, helpless, gasping from Roxanne's kick. I hit him a few shots while she spurred me on.

"That's it, Frankie, hit him again!"

"The gun," I grunted between blows. "Get the gun!"

"I can't. He's laying on it."

"Shit."

"Hurry!" she urged. "They're coming."

I could hear the slamming of car doors, footfalls coming closer. The guy under me was either unconscious or too comfortable to move. I tried to roll him off the gun but he wouldn't budge.

"Hold them off," I called to her. "And for Chrissakes, forget the bag!"

She'd managed to retrieve the damn thing and was holding it to her chest as if it contained a bomb instead of money. She looked more like a wacko terrorist on self-destruct than a young woman with confused priorities. But Roxanne didn't need a bomb. She had long legs and courage enough for both of us.

She discarded the bag and her shoes, and went at them with the ferocity of a Bengal tiger, stopping the driver with a kick to the gonads. He went down and she dove head first into the arms of Jake's captor. They hit the ground, legs entangled, arms and fists flailing.

Meanwhile, I was down on my haunches, using my legs and feet to roll two hundred pounds of dead meat off a very live shotgun. By the time I got it, the fight was over. The tiger had been tamed.

"Drop it," the guy said.

He had Roxanne in a hammerlock, forcing her forward by applying upward pressure to the arm bent awkwardly behind her. The higher he pushed the more pain he inflicted. Rising on her toes, Roxanne yelped but shook it off gamely. Her karate instructor would have been proud of her. I know I was.

"Don't do it, Frankie," she said. "They'll kill us anyway."

If I had a pistol I could have picked him off without hitting Roxanne. But a scattergun was never meant for small targets.

"Let her go," I said. "You can have the money. Let her go."

"We'll take her *and* the money," came a voice from behind.

I knew who it was without looking. But like a fool I turned anyway. I was halfway around when my chin met his fist.

8

It was a pleasant nap, an idle refuge from thugs, guns and wild car chases. A mild ocean breeze caressed my cheeks. The rising sun conjured dreams of a tropical isle. Roxanne and I were resting peacefully on the soft coral sand of a lazy lagoon. If only I could have stayed there.

"You all right?" said an anxious, disembodied voice.

Groaning, I rolled onto my side, clasped my hands in prayer, tucked them under my face, and went back to sleep.

"Hey!" said the voice. "Have you been drinking?"

"Go 'way, James. There's no school today."

"You're right about that, Mac. Now get up. I want to smell your breath."

I sat up. In two seconds I went from REM sleep to stark reality. It was the uniform that did it. The gray hat, black boots, the smell of gun oil from a sleek leather holster.

"*Now* you come," I mumbled to the squatting cop, his face was so close I could have kissed him without puckering.

He took a whiff and said, "You're not drunk." He seemed more confused than disappointed. Which was perfectly understandable under the circumstances.

He helped me up and waited for the explanation.

My chin hurt like hell but my head was clearing up and so were my eyes. Unfortunately. With the exception of one perplexed cop, there was no one else in sight.

Years ago, on rainy days in Akron when there was nothing to do but get in our mother's hair, James and I would pass the time with a game called "Bullshit." We'd make up stories, putting our hero in all kinds of perilous fixes. The idea was to leave him hanging by a thread, then save his life through the sheer power of adolescent imagery. Most times it was a friendly pterodactyl that swooped down in the nick of time, using its powerful talons to scoop him up and drop him off, safe and sound. More than a passtime, our game became an art. I reached deep into my stash of childhood bullshit.

"I don't know what happened, Officer. One minute I'm driving along, next thing I know you're waking me up."

He wrinkled his nose like something foul had just wafted down from Secaucus.

"Your license and registration," he said.

He checked them out and chatted me up at the same time. "You don't know what happened," he said. "You just pulled over, got out and went to sleep on the side of the road."

"I guess so," I said.

"You don't recall the blowout?"

"Blowout?"

"Your back tire," he said. "It's blown to pieces."

I wrinkled my nose like his and for a while we looked like a pair of horny rabbits in a mating ritual. Of course I knew then what had happened. They'd grabbed the money and taken Roxanne, shooting out my tire to make sure I wouldn't get frisky and chase them. Why they'd abduct Roxanne, I had no idea. Or why they had left me alive.

Taking my arm, the cop led me to the back of my car. It was listing badly, the result of a shotgun blast that had left the tire looking like shredded wheat and the rear quarter panel like swiss cheese. He didn't look too closely, thank God.

I didn't dare relate any of this to the cop. If he didn't buy amnesia, he'd never go for the truth. "You must have been going pretty fast," the cop said, eyeing me. "What did you do, bang your chin on the wheel? Your jaw is swollen."

"I don't remember."

"Look," he said, "this is New Jersey not New York. Maybe you can bullshit cops up there, but not here. If I can't give you a ticket for speeding, I ought to pull you in on general principles. Now fix this tire and get the hell out of here before you fall asleep again. You got a spare?"

I nodded.

"That you remember, eh? New Yorkers," he said, shaking his head in disgust. "You're all crazy."

"I'll be out of here in ten minutes," I told him.

He straightened his hat, adjusted his gloves and said, "See that you are."

It wasn't until I'd changed the tire and was putting things back in the trunk that I realized Betso's boys had made a serious mistake. They'd snatched a bag, all right. But the one they took was filled with laundry.

9

I kept telling myself that Betso's loss was our gain. Mine and Roxanne's. He wouldn't kill her without the money and he couldn't get the money until he came to me. I figured to trade the money for Roxanne. Until that happened we'd be safe, though not very sound. I knew damn well he'd take us out once he had what he wanted.

I needed help. If anyone out there cared about me, the time to prove it was now.

In my mind I ran a list of prospective champions, someone to pick up the gauntlet of Fat Alfie Betso. My choices were sparse.

There was James, of course. He'd grab the first plane out of Akron without being asked if he knew I needed him. But my brother was a babe in the woods, a lawyer whose expertise wasn't criminals but decedents. He wrote wills and settled estates. He knew about executing trusts, not people. Besides, I loved him too much.

I did have one semi-hostile acquaintance in the N.Y.P.D. Detective Lieutenant Grimm. He had gotten his promotion by busting the guy he worked for. In all modesty, he couldn't have done it without me.

It was damn depressing to think that there were only two people on the right side of the law who could help me. More depressing were the choices it left me.

Had the game been straight, I could have gone to Scarlo's boss, Manny Adonis. While Adonis might have extorted half my business in exchange for the help, it was a chance I would have taken, had I not seen Jake's cowering face in the back of that Lincoln. Jake had dealt from the bottom and Roxanne had paid for the service. My guess was that she intended to rip me off once we got to New York. There was no way Manny Adonis would intercede to save a scam artist who had burned a syndicate loan shark.

Roxanne had used me and I had every right in the world to let her go down for it. Except I couldn't. I couldn't just sit by and allow people to kill her if there was a chance to stop it.

But Adonis would never help me if he knew I'd cheated Betso. It was that fucking code of honor these people wore on the lapels of their five-hundred-dollar suits. Damn. More likely, he'd furnish Betso with a grave site, some shovels and a team of diggers to help plant me. Reluctantly, I scratched Adonis from the list.

That left me with any number of paid buttons who would gladly jump in if the price was right and I went along with their *modus operandi*, which, when reduced to its lowest common denominator, would be to waste Betso and keep the money for themselves. My goal wasn't to get Betso killed but to save Roxanne and me from such a fate. The more I thought about it, the more I realized that I had no choice at all. I'd have to deal with Betso on my own.

My first order of business therefore, was to put business aside. Broken ovens and faulty pipes had taken a considerable dip on my list of priorities. Which was the reason I didn't go to work but drove directly to my loft, where I waited all afternoon and late into the evening.

I planned on hiding the money in the restaurant, in a concealed compartment under the bar where the only thing concealed at the moment was an unregistered .45 automatic. I'd bought the gun more for reassurance than protection, keeping both the compartment and the weapon a secret even from the bartender, Sally. Not that Sally was squeamish about guns. It made me wish I had her with me as I nerved myself to leave. If not Sally, then certainly the .45.

It was only a ten minute drive to the restaurant. I could have walked but the trip covered streets you'd hate to use even in broad daylight. Crowned by shadows from the 59th Street Bridge, the entire route, from loft to Fontana's, was one desolate expanse of warehouse and industrial buildings, set against a backdrop of the richest residences in Manhattan, just across the river. Next to balconied high-rise buildings nestled three-story townhouses. On my side of the river, aside from dogs, cats, and rats, the only forms of life were muggers, and the occasional hired killer. Not where you'd want to be at four a.m. Especially with three hundred fifty grand in your gym bag.

I didn't wait around when I hit the street. My car was right out front and I dove into it without looking, started up and took off with a screech that cut the stillness. If Betso's men were nearby, they'd be on me before I reached the corner. Nobody showed. To make sure, I made a few wrong turns and drove very slowly all the way to the restaurant. I passed it by, then doubled back, keeping a sharp eye for anything out of place. The street looked normal: dark and deserted.

I parked a block away to keep my car out of sight, then hot-footed back to the restaurant. The front was bathed in the light of a street lamp, so I went around the side and let myself in through the kitchen. Once inside I needed no lights. I knew every inch of floor space and I used that familiarity to cut a swift, silent path to the bar.

The compartment was under the cash register, in back of one of the cabinets Sally used to store booze. The idea was to press a button along the inside vertical molding, then watch as the panel retracted. The boys from Local 3 had charged a bundle for this small toy.

I pressed the button. I couldn't see but I could hear. The door slid back and I offered a silent vow to never again badmouth organized labor.

The compartment was the size of a small locker you see at airports and bus depots: big enough for a bowling ball, an attaché case, a gym bag. I moved the bottles aside to make an opening wide enough for the bag, reached in and groped for the .45. It was a heavy son of a bitch and carrying it around wasn't something I looked forward to. But Betso's troops had shotguns, for God's sake. I tucked the .45 in my belt and wondered if perhaps I shouldn't trade up for a frigging Uzi.

Pressing the button, I listened to the panel slide shut. Satisfied that all was secure, I went back to the office, opened the cot, placed the gun under my pillow, and fell into sleep.

Roxanne and I were boarding a plane for Brazil. The flight attendant was Carmine Genovese. He checked our tickets, grinned and opened the door to the cockpit. Behind the controls sat Fat Alfie Betso.

"We got a problem, Captain," said Flight Attendant Carmine. "We're going to Brazil but these two yo-yo's got tickets to Akron."

Betso turned, chuckled and said, "No sweat. We're over Ohio. Just open the door and push 'em out."

There was a strange tickling sensation in the pit of my stomach. I was falling to earth, arms and legs outstretched, flying free like a sky diver, studying the ground with bemused interest as it drew closer and closer.

When I opened my eyes Sally Plunk was standing over me. "What day is it?" I said.

She shook her head. "Oh, brother. Must have been some trip. It's Friday, Rip Van Winkle. Our busy night, remember? Or have you given up the restaurant business for gambling and other forms of ill-gotten gains?"

"Go 'way," I said. I turned over and felt something hard beneath my cheek. I reached under the pillow, felt the .45. "Oh shit," I mumbled.

Sally said, "It's five p.m. We let you sleep, now get up and earn your money."

I rubbed the sleep from my eyes. "Any calls?"

"Too many. Hey," she said, "go home, grab a shower and get down here before anyone sees you. One look at you and we'll lose the dinner crowd to McDonald's."

"Frig the dinner crowd. Tell me who called."

I must have sounded worse than I looked because Sally got serious real quick. She pulled a chair from the desk and sat down beside the cot.

"Four calls," she said. "Scarlo . . . said welcome back and thanks for changing his luck. A chick named Linda Dorsey. Long distance. Sounded upset when you weren't available. Said she'd call back. Scarlo again. Wants you to be his guest at dinner tonight. Said thanks for changing his luck. Last but not least,

Linda Dorsey. She'll be here at seven o'clock. Now, you mind telling me what's going down?"

"Nothing," I said. "Just gas up the car and point it toward Brazil."

Sally laughed. It was half-hearted. She'd been around me long enough to sense trouble. "Wanna talk?"

"Can't, Sally. Just watch the place for me. I'll be in and out, but even when I'm in, I'll be out."

"Crystal clear." She sighed. "I don't know what happened in A.C., but I'll bet my next paycheck there's a broad behind it somewhere. Is it the one who keeps calling—Ms. Dorsey?"

"Never heard of her."

"I'll bet. Go on, get outta here."

I cleared the menu with the chefs, then went home to shower and change.

I was going to take the gun with me but reconsidered when I thought about the downside risk. Getting caught with a concealed weapon would cost me my liquor license. After months of aggravation, cajoling and payoffs, losing it now would be something I could never explain to James.

There were practical reasons too. Without a holster, the only place to carry a .45 was behind my back inside my belt. It fit all right, but it made sitting down a bitch. To say nothing of how difficult it would be to draw in a hurry. By the time I fumbled it free, I'd be toes up in the street. The .45 stayed in the office while I dashed home, cleaned myself up, and returned.

It was 7:15 by the time I got back. Once again I entered via the kitchen. Only this time it wasn't quiet. Mayhem was more like it. Clanging pots, hissing pans, shouting, cursing, a cacophony befitting a gaggle of inmates greeted me. I ducked inside, cut swiftly through steam and spattering grease, and went directly to the office. Someone was waiting for me.

I closed the door behind me.

"Linda Dorsey," she said.

The voice had the same husky intonation, the eyes were hazel but the hair was different: blonde instead of auburn, a loose wave in place of the perm. Her features were close to Roxanne's except for a mole on the right side of her mouth.

"What can I help you with?" I said.

"Are you Frank Fontana?"

"Yeah," I said.

"Roxanne is my sister," she said. "Her real name is Rose Ann Dorsey. I've flown all the way from Denver on one hour's notice. I've come here to see you because my sister asked me to. She's in serious trouble, Mr. Fontana. I'm tired and worried. I need sleep and an aspirin. But most of all, I need help."

If she needed help, what did I need? One member of her family in my life was more than enough, thank you. She'd been sitting at the desk, chair turned toward the door. Her legs were crossed under a gray linen skirt, hands folded primly in her lap.

"How did you find me?" I said.

"Your hotel registration: F. Fontana, care of Fontana's, Queens, New York."

"You called Bally's?" There was no way the hotel would have just released that information to a caller.

"No," she said. "Rose Ann told me. She knows someone at the desk. He checked it out."

"Right," I said. "Now what?"

"You got something in Atlantic City," she said. "She told me to say that if you'd return it, she'd be okay and no one would bother you."

"What else did she say?"

"Nothing. Except that you were a decent guy and you'd understand."

"Define decent guy," I said.

"I'm running out of patience, Mr. Fontana. I've told you why I'm here. Are you going to help me, or not?"

"What happens if I don't?"

She rubbed her forehead like I was giving her the headache.

"My sister's always been a flake," she said. "Her idea of fun is full contact karate. I don't *know* what will happen if you don't help. But she's never asked me for anything in her life. Now she has, so it means it's very serious. Are you a thief, Mr. Fontana?"

"Worse," I said. "I'm naive. I let myself get conned by your sister. I'm not about to do it again, Miss Dorsey. Now if you don't mind, I've got work to do."

"You won't help me," she said, rubbing her brow.

I studied her for a long moment.

"How about dinner, Miss Dorsey? It will ease your headache. I hear the food's pretty good in this place."

"Thank you," she said.

I smiled and called for Joanne.

We had dinner in my office. It wasn't exactly romantic but there were no interruptions. She talked freely and candidly. By the time she'd finished I knew more about Linda Dorsey than about my ex-wife.

It didn't take long to see that Linda Dorsey possessed all the qualities sorely lacking in her sister. Linda was a rock: soft-spoken, level headed, forthright. She had poise and a strong sense of direction. In a word, class—something else I wasn't used to.

She told me she'd been married before, that her ex-husband was a lieutenant colonel and taught aerodynamics at the Air Force Academy in Colorado Springs. A real heady guy.

"I met him in Plattsburg, New York," she said. "I was attending college up there and he was stationed at the base. I was twenty-one and he was a captain. My sister had gone through a pair of husbands by then. Our parents were never too thrilled with her choices, so naturally, when I told them about Jeffrey, they were delighted.

"We're from Yonkers originally, middle class all the way. It never bothered me but Rose Ann was another story. She hated Yonkers. 'It's too nine to five,' she said. 'I want a place that's five to nine.' She went to Puerto Rico on vacation one summer and never came back. She married a dealer from one of the casinos."

"His name wasn't Jake by any chance."

"Ramon," she said. "It lasted three months. Just long enough for her to get caught fooling around. Ramon threw her out and she picked up with a gambler named Danny DeSimone."

"Danny D.?"

"Yeah, you know him? A real charmer. Needless to say, that didn't last much longer than her first marriage. They couldn't make it as husband and wife. Once that was put out of the way, they got along swimmingly. The one thing they have in common is an addiction to gambling. I doubt she ever loved Danny. If anything, she loved his type—fast and loose. Maybe that's the reason she went for you."

"When's the last time she saw him?" I said.

"I have no idea. But they keep in touch, I know that. Why?"

"She told me she was being kept by a married man. Would that be Danny?"

"Definitely not," Linda said. "They're just friends. They gamble together. Junkets and like that. I know Danny. He couldn't make the payments on somebody like her. No, she told you the truth."

"Score one for Roxanne," I said. "Who is the guy she's seeing, do you know?"

"I have no idea. But he's got money and influence. An attorney or stockbroker I think. He treats my sister well enough, I guess. Still, she comes second, if you know what I mean."

"What about you?" I said. "What are you doing in Denver?"

"Struggling. I have a small business. A boutique. I always liked Denver. At least I did until the oil glut. The city's not what it used to be. My ex and I spent a great deal of time there. He has family nearby and it's not too far from the academy. After we divorced I moved to Denver and opened the shop. That was four years ago."

"What happened?" I said.

"With the marriage?"

I nodded.

She sighed heavily. "He's a good man but he loves the service too much. It's not the kind of love a woman competes with. Also I couldn't take all the moving. Anyway, it's over." She poured out two cups of coffee, gave me one and said, "What's going on here, Frank?"

I took a deep breath and let it out slowly. "Yeah," I said, "I want to be honest with you, Linda. But . . . something doesn't compute here. If Roxanne knew where to find me, why didn't she call me herself? Why drag you into it?"

"I don't understand," she said. "What the hell are you talking about?"

What I was talking about was something I couldn't talk about. I kept wondering why Betso's men had taken Roxanne away and why they'd left me there in one piece. It made no sense. Betso wanted *me* more than Roxanne. He told me so. Why only take her? Unless Betso didn't figure in this. But if those guys weren't Betso's, whose were they? Had to be Roxanne's. She knew he would find out that our game was rigged, that he'd come after us quickly and efficiently. All she had to do was rip me off before it happened. She disappears and I'm left holding. Except the bag I was holding had all the money. As Roxanne would say, Mistake.

But she'd fought like hell against our attackers. Or was I totally conned?

"Please," I said. "Tell me when she called you. I want to know exactly what she said. Word for word."

She drank some coffee while she thought it over. "About twelve-thirty, I think. It was just before lunch. She hadn't called me in months so I was surprised to hear from her." She paused a moment and looked up at the ceiling. "Let's see. I'm trying to recall exactly what she said. She'd spent a few days in Atlantic City. 'I met this guy,' she said. 'A decent guy, for a change.'" She gave me a look of suspicion.

"Go on."

"She said the two of you had won a bundle in a poker game. I said that was great and she said, 'Not really. Most of it's in markers.' She said you promised to collect them in New York from a man named Betso. When I asked her why she didn't come back with you, she said she couldn't. She got vague. Said her guy was coming down to meet her and she had to be there when he arrived. Apparently he's very possessive."

"How did she sound?" I said. "Was she worried, frightened?"

"Rose Ann's a very up-beat person," Linda said. "She didn't tell me how much you'd won but she was very nervous about it. Then she told me what she wanted."

"And?"

"It's hard to explain," Linda said. "She didn't sound upset, not at first. But after she'd told me what happened, she was close to panic. She said this man, Betso, had come to her room after you left. He was quite angry. 'Vicious' was the word she used. He thought he'd been cheated. Demanded his markers and the return of all the money he'd lost. Of course she couldn't accommodate. When she told him you'd taken everything with you, he went crazy. Trashed the room and slapped her around. He's holding her, Frank."

"Yes," I said. "I know."

"You know?" Linda paused. "What the fuck!"

"Take it easy."

She flushed. "Easy! This isn't a game we're playing."

"I'm aware of that."

"Is that so? You sit here flirting with me over dinner, wasting time, when you know Rose Ann—"

"Calm down," I said. "I'm not wasting time. I'm buying some. Until Betso gets what he wants, he won't hurt your sister. It's after I'm worried about."

"Sure," Linda said. "You're safe in your office. And I sit here reciting stuff you already know. You tell me he won't hurt her but he's already beaten her up. Now give me those markers, Mr. Fontana! Or so help me—"

"Or you'll go out and get your sister killed, is what you'll do. Now listen to me. There are no markers. No paper. What I've got is cash. Three hundred and fifty big ones."

"She told me—"

"Yeah, I know." I held up my hand. "Three hundred fifty grand, Linda. You know your sister better than I do. With that much at stake, would she trust a man she's known for two lousy days?"

I waited while Linda pushed that question through gray matter. It didn't take her long.

"No," she said, looking away. "She wouldn't."

"Then you agree something's fishy."

"I agree." She nodded. "What do we do?"

"Finish the story. What happened after she said Betso slapped her around?"

"He told her to get someone to pick up the . . . money from you. Someone she trusts."

"Lucky you," I said. "You get the money. Then what?"

"I go to her apartment and wait for a call."

"Where's that?"

"East 78th Street. That's where my stuff is. I got the key from the doorman. It's a high rise apartment, very posh."

"Her married friend pays the freight?"

She nodded. "I think so."

"Well," I said, "one thing for sure. You can't go back there. They might grab you and I'll have you both to worry about."

"Worry about?" Linda said.

"Yeah. Now I'm going to tell you how it really went down."

I told her what happened on the Garden State. How we fought and lost. How they nabbed her sister and took a bag of my laundry by mistake. I kept the nasty notions to myself.

She was greatly puzzled by the kidnapping. Which made it unanimous.

"I'm sorry," she said. "I know you're trying to help. But you're all alone. What can you do against a man like Betso?"

I still wasn't convinced those were Betso's boys out there, but if they were, they'd be plenty confused.

I smiled. "Find a man tougher than Betso. Matter of fact," I said, remembering Scarlo's dinner invitation as I checked my watch, "I believe there's one at the bar right now.

"You look worried."

"Yeah," I said absently. Until now, Fontana's had never seen a gun drawn in anger but it wouldn't take much to turn my place into a war zone.

76

10

A bartender I knew had a saying: My head tells me one thing but my mind tells me something else.

I went to the bar looking for Scarlo. My head told me he'd be there, my mind told me he wouldn't. My mind proved right.

I pulled Sally aside. "What happened to Scarlo?"

"Don't know," she said, harried, sweaty.

It was a typical Friday night, crowded and noisy. It should have made me happy but it didn't and I wasn't.

"Said he'd be back."

"What time did he say?"

She eyed the digital above the register. "Hour. You here to pitch in or bullshit? If it's bullshit, clear out. I'm busy."

Helluva way to treat the boss, I thought. But dedication's a rare commodity in this business. Sally had it and the best thing I could do was let her perform. I cleared out.

Actually I went to work. If that's what you call cruising the tables, playing ambassador, spreading good will, entertaining ill-founded complaints, killing time till Scarlo showed.

I smiled and nodded for a good hour and a half. By the time the rush ended I felt like one of those dolls with springs for a neck. I was about to call it a night when Manny Adonis made his entrance.

I could tell it was Manny by the sudden hush that fell over the place. From Bedlam to the Public Library in one second. Heads turned, eyes dropped, fingers twiddled. A path opened, a passageway for the undisputed crown prince.

As usual, it was Manny's mainstays who cleared the way. Girdled by a half dozen orangutans in dark suits, Manny sauntered regally toward my number one booth, which, if it wasn't empty, would have been, lickety split.

The orangutans waited for Manny to slide in safely before taking their places. All but one. He was the largest of the group. But he had a friendly face and, when he turned to the crowd, he smiled and nodded. No trouble, was the sign. Carry on, was the message.

The joint picked up where it left off.

I'd been in the back, near the kitchen, watching Manny's grand entrance. I was still standing there when the big guy spotted me. He ambled toward me and I realized he had one more message to deliver.

I cloaked my anxiety with an ambassadorial nonchalance and proceeded to cut him off at the pass. Even at six feet, I looked straight up at the guy. He said, "Mr. Adonis wants to see ya."

As if I didn't know.

He shifted his bulk, waited for me to pass, then lumbered after me.

I tried to count the number of times Manny Adonis had adorned the half-moon booth he now occupied. Ten, fifteen maybe. We had had a number of conversations but they'd always been casual and had I been the initiator in every case. Never once had he summoned me. I smelled something in the air and it wasn't coming from the river.

Adonis would have made it big in anything. He was that kind of guy. Early sixties, tall, handsome, well-groomed, with salt and pepper hair combed straight back off a low forehead. He looked like an ad for confidence and acted like the chairman of the board, a senior partner, chief resident. You would never picture him driving a truck, mowing a lawn, or drinking beer from a bottle, even cursing.

Any pool shark will tell you that position is nine tenths of the game. I didn't know Adonis very well, but I was confident Mr. Adonis appreciated the concept.

He raised his eyes from the menu as I approached.

I said, amiably, "How are you tonight, Mr. Adonis?"

"Hungry."

For what? I wondered.

"We've got a veal marsala tonight," I told him. "Very good. Had it myself awhile ago."

He cocked his head and regarded me with a narrow stare. "You don't look unwell," he said. "so I'll have it."

This brought a chuckle from his boys—a deep rumbling, like an approaching subway. When the train stopped, Adonis said, "If it's that good you can have it again."

He flicked his head to one side. I thought it was a tic; his escort knew better. They got up as one and moved out. I took a seat and prepared for my second supper. I didn't mind eating another meal, provided it wasn't my last. We ordered the veal and a bottle of Bordeaux.

He waited for me to pour the wine, then said, "I want to ask you something."

I wondered how he'd react if I'd simply said, Sorry, no questions tonight. But his dark eyes had me pinned to my seat. "Sure," I said, "anything you want."

"You had some problem with Candy Gizzo?"

I shrugged. "It's history."

"I'm sure you've thought about it," he said.

"I have."

"What would you have done if he hadn't died just when he did? Would you've fought him?"

Silence.

The only person who could have put Candy Gizzo away was yours truly. The wiseguys knew it, the law knew it, the whole fucking city knew it. No one knew it better than me. For several weeks I'd lived on borrowed time, staring at the suponea and scanning travel brochures to obscure places like Botswana, Cape Verde, Upper Volta. Gizzo's timely demise had gotten me off the hook. Now, it seemed, I was back on it.

"No," I finally said.

Adonis smiled sardonically.

"I'll admit I wanted to," I added quickly. "I mean he was trying to kill me, wasn't he? But there's no way I could have gotten him."

"From what I hear, he had cause."

"It wasn't me," I said. "I'm not crazy enough to squeeze a man like Gizzo."

"That's right," Adonis said. "I believe it was a lady, and that friend of yours, Candy's nephew."

"That guy always was a jerk."

"Not any more," he said.

With a shaky hand I brought the bordeaux to my lips. Or tried to. It splashed on the way up, spilling down the glass, over my hand, onto the white tablecloth. Very suave.

Adonis seemed amused. He reached over and calmly patted the stain with his napkin.

"Here comes the food," I said.

It was Joanne's table. She placed the meals quickly, asked the perfunctory questions: Was everything all right? Was there anything else she could do? Then beat it like the bright girl she was.

Adonis handled his meal the way I assumed he handled his business: methodically, checking everything carefully before trying it out. He turned the meat over, sniffed and pōked it. Once he was satisfied, he seemed to savor every bite, placing the knife across the dish while he brought the food to his mouth with a fork held in his left hand. He'd swallow, down it with wine, then talk.

"Habits," he said again. "Drinking's a habit. Smoking. Even gambling. I didn't know you were a gambler, Fontana."

"I'm not."

"Lying's a habit, too," he said quickly. He placed the knife carefully on his dish, chewed, drank. He said, "It's one habit I can't abide."

"I'm not lying," I said.

"Oh. You tell me you're not a gambler. But there you are in A.C., busting a game big enough to retire guys like you. How do you account for that, Fontana?"

It's amazing how quickly word gets around in the underworld. Especially when you consider how tight-mouthed these people are. A guy gets whacked in San Diego and ten minutes later it's all over Brooklyn.

"I could tell you," I said, "but you'd never believe it."

"Give it your best shot." Adonis wiped his lips.

There was no sense in lying, that much I knew. He would never have asked me if he didn't already know what took place. But something wasn't right here. The game was fixed. Betso knew it, which meant Adonis knew it. So why question me about it? Was he feeling me out for some other purpose? From what I knew of Manny Adonis, the answer had to be yes.

I told him the story, picking it up from the time I met Roxanne. How we met, Carmine's involvement, and the great car chase. Roxanne's abduction.

He listened intently. No questions, no interruptions. When I finished, he shook his head. If anything, he seemed amused.

"You mean to tell me," he said, grinning, "that after all that, they never got the money?"

"That's right."

"I'm glad those guys don't work for me." He sighed heavily. "But that doesn't alter the situation. You're in a lot of trouble, Fontana. Guess you know that."

"I was used," I said.

"Were you? This girl, what's her name . . . Roxanne? You think she's behind it?"

Now I really had a problem. Tell him yes and Roxanne is dead. Lie to him and *I'm* dead. What I needed was a fall guy. A guy like . . .

"Carmine Genovese," I said. "It had to be him. A set up between him and Jake."

"The dealer?" Adonis said.

"That's right. I mean it figures. Carmine didn't have stake money. He lures me into the game knowing he'll rip me off. He even tried to snatch the money from me on the way out. When it didn't work, he sent those guys after us. They roughed her up pretty good, Mr. Adonis. Would they do that if she was in on it?"

"Maybe," he said.

He took a bite of veal, chewed, drank.

Then he said, "But you thought it was Betso's crew. That's what you told me. You change your mind?"

"No. I mean if it wasn't Carmine, it had to be Betso. I thought maybe you knew."

Apparently the statement killed Manny's appetite. He dropped his fork, pushed his plate away and said, "How the hell would I know? I'm here talking to you. If I knew, would I talk to you?"

"I guess not. But you knew I was there, about the game and all. I just figured . . . Shit, I don't know."

"Yeah," Adonis said. "You just figured Betso picked up a phone and told me all about it. What do you know about Alfie Betso?"

"Not much. He's a shy out of Jersey City."

Manny studied me for a moment, smiled, and said, "I see you don't spend much time in Jersey City. If Betso's a shylock, then what am I?"

There it was. Betso wasn't just a connected guy, he had his own family, for Christ's sake. Betso in Jersey City, Adonis in Brooklyn. Who was it said, Hope springs eternal? Point him out so I can kick him in the ass.

I wanted to look Adonis in the eye but it was a hard thing to do.

I was staring down at my hands, gathering courage, when he said, "Let me tell you what you're up against, Fontana. Look at me!"

I looked.

He seemed calm enough. Like a judge. "It's not only Betso," he said. "It's the whole fucking combine. Speaking for myself, I couldn't care less what happened to Betso. It's between you and him. Personally, I hope you beat him. But know this. He puts out the word, I'll have to step in. You hear what I'm saying, Fontana?"

In a voice I'd never heard before, I said, "Yes."

Adonis looked away. "Only reason you're sitting here is because Betso's hands are tied. This is my territory. Whatever goes down here, goes through me. So far nothing's been said. You know why?" His eyes came back to me.

By this time I was too numb to speak in any voice. I shook my head no.

"It's his money. I give him help, he has to pay to get it back. Would you pay for something that's already yours? You played cards with the man. What do you think?"

The only thing I thought was that I was getting drunk. The combination of wine and fear had my head spinning. So far the two components were in perfect balance. I took more wine to tip the scales.

My tongue responded by getting thicker. Slurring, I said, "Why are you telling me this? I mean what do you care what happens to me?"

"Normally I wouldn't," he said, casually. "If you cheat, you deserve what you get. But I don't see you in this, Fontana. It's not the kind of move a guy like you would make."

He paused and I thought Manny Adonis a very astute fellow.

He said, "Let's just say I have a personal interest."

Personal interest? Was that good or bad? I didn't know but I jumped all over it.

"Then help me, for Chrissake. If you believe me, you can make Betso believe. You can straighten it out. I'll give him his fucking money."

"And the girl?"

"No," I said. "No girl, no money."

He shook his head. "Doesn't work that way. You cheat, you have to pay for it. It's how it is."

"I can't let her go down," I said.

Adonis frowned but didn't say anything.

"So what should I do?" I said.

He shrugged. "You'll think of something. You beat Gizzo didn't you?"

"You mean I survived."

He raised his hand for the check. "Tell you what," he said. "If you get out of this, come see me. Could be we'll do some business." He chuckled. "Meanwhile, it should be fun to watch."

"Yeah," I said. "A million laughs."

He shook his head. "You take these things too personally."

11

Adonis left me sitting in the booth. Alone. Apparently he had more faith in me than I had in myself. Which wasn't saying a helluva lot.

What I had to do now was analyze the conversation. Or lack of it. I've been around long enough to know that when wiseguys talk it's not what they say that matters. It's what they don't say. Slight omissions, innuendo. The hidden message.

That I was safe from Adonis for a while was clear. Why I was safe was the hidden message. I have a personal interest, he'd said. Now *there* was a message with a hundred hidden meanings. I tried to pinpoint the most logical. What I came up with was Fat Alfie.

I had to figure that Betso was as big in New Jersey as Adonis was in Brooklyn. In short, counterparts in the same organization. I pictured Manny and Betso on the same team, at the same table, hammering out issues of import: territorial disputes, payoffs, overlapping responsibilities. Manny and Betso, the matador and the bull.

Suddenly the hidden message seemed obvious: Manny's plan was to eighty-six Betso, wipe him out as a rival. Fine. But how? Jesus, I thought. Through me, that's how!

But did he expect me to kill the man? Not likely. So what the hell was it? How did I fit into Adonis's plan? Talk about tangled webs. Was there one accountant in this whole goddamn city that had problems like these?

Ignoring my customers and their how-you-doing-Frankies, I hauled myself from the booth and went back to my office to check on Linda. I had told her to stay put, and what do I get? A note:

Dear Frank,
Went to the city to pick up my things. Be back shortly.
Linda.

Great! While Linda picks up her things, Betso picks up Linda.

I grabbed the Manhattan phone book and checked for Ducharme on East 78th. To my surprise I found the listing. I dialed.

"Hi," came Roxanne's throaty voice. "I'm not home right now. If you owe me money, leave your name and number. Otherwise, call back."

"Goddamn machines," I muttered. The answering machine beeped and I said, "Linda, if you're there, pick up."

I waited. Nothing, except another beep. "Shit."

I destroyed the note and ran my fingers across the desk. The .45 was locked in the top drawer where I'd left it before going home to change. Maybe it was time to take it for a walk. I opened the drawer and gazed at the gun. Slick, it glistened in the light of the gooseneck lamp like some shiny black tool.

No, I thought, not yet. I closed the drawer and locked it.

"You there, Frankie?" Sally Plunk's tired face peered at me from behind the partially opened door.

Whirling, I scowled at her. "Did you see her leave?"

Nonplussed, she said, "Who?"

"Linda Dorsey. The woman who was supposed to be in this frigging office waiting for me."

She shrugged. "That's the way it goes, Frank. Win a few, lose a few. Could be you're losing your charm."

"Don't be cute, Sally. I'm in no mood."

"Well excuse me," she said, indignantly. "I didn't know girl watching was part of the job description. You told me to take charge tonight and that's what I did. I might say that I busted my ass in the process. So," she added, "you wanna start over?"

Sally Plunk was more to me than a valued employee. She was the only person I'd ever known in this business who wasn't out to beat the system, or the boss. I trusted Sally implicitly. More than that, I cherished our friendship.

"Come in here a minute, will you, Sal?"

She smirked but stepped inside, closing the door behind her.

"Have I ever kissed you?" I said.

"A half dozen times," she said. "Every New Year's Eve for the past six years."

"I don't mean that."

"Oh, Christ," she said. "If I'd known it would come down to this I would've chained that broad to your desk. Keep your distance, Fontana. I like you but it don't include swappin' spit."

I laughed. "I'm trying to apologize."

"Then say you're sorry and keep your whatever to yourself."

"I'm sorry."

"Forgiven."

We stood there, trading those dumb smiles of conciliation, when someone knocked on the door. A flustered Joanne.

"Sorry to bother you," she said. "But I was told if I didn't get you out, he'd break the door down."

I looked at Sally. "Don't tell me."

"I won't," she replied, gesturing toward Joanne. "She will."

"The Petrones are with him," Joanne said hurriedly, squinting. "He's really pissed off. Know what I mean?"

I glanced at Sally. "Thought you said he was in a good mood."

She looked at her watch. "That was hours ago. A lot can happen in six hours."

"Tell Mr. Scarlo I'll be right out."

Relieved, Joanne scampered away. Sally hesitated—"Be careful."—and followed.

I headed out to find Johnny Scarlo and walked into a wall of flesh. Sid Petrone.

"Inside," he said, shoving me backward.

I stumbled across the cot and remained there while Petrone moved aside and Scarlo walked in. He looked for all the world like a man who hated life, liberty, and the pursuit of any kind of happiness.

"Close the door." He motioned vaguely to Sid. "Stay outside till I need ya."

Sid closed the door and I was trapped in a twelve by fifteen foot box I had laughingly called my sanctuary. Scarlo didn't beat around the bush. "What's going on with you and Adonis?"

I countered with a stumper of my own. "What's going on with you?"

I was sitting on the cot, looking up at him, my face about even with his hand. A perfect target. I braced for a lateral strike but Scarlo went straight at me. The heel of his hand caught the top of my forehead. My head snapped back and my eyes slammed shut. When they opened again, there were more stars in my office than the Hayden Planetarium.

"You had a sit down with Adonis," he said. "Why? What did he say?"

I shook away the the Big Dipper and gazed blankly at Scarlo.

"Don't make me smack you around," he said. "It might get outta hand. You're gonna tell me anyway so you might as well do it while you still got teeth."

I ran my tongue over my molars and proceeded to tell him the saga of Fat Alfie Betso. I wrapped it up with a recap of what Adonis had told me, emphasizing that his boss had promised a definite hands-off policy.

Unfazed by that last remark, Scarlo said, "What he say about the card game?"

"He found it amusing. Especially when he heard they didn't get the money. I got the feeling it's Betso he really wants."

"He don't want him more than me," Scarlo said. "That prick's been a thorn in our side for a long time. Always pushin' his fat face where it don't belong. Manny won't touch the fuck until the house falls in. But I will."

He snatched my collar and pulled me up. "And you're gonna help me, Fontana." He pushed me back. "You help me and I'll help you. That's fair, ain't it?"

I didn't know Scarlo as a child, but I would guess he didn't play fair even in kindergarten.

"Sure," I said. "That's fair. Until Adonis finds out. He made himself very clear—he's not getting involved. That includes you, doesn't it? You work for the man."

"I'm doin' this for *him*," Scarlo said. "When it's all over he'll thank me. Gimme a bonus, maybe."

"Yeah," I said. "The two of us. Silver bullets."

"Don't worry 'bout that," he said. "Any bullets, they're gonna come from me. I'm the one you gotta worry about."

He was right about that. "There's still something we haven't talked about," I said.

Scarlo grinned. "The money."

"The girl. The one they snatched. I have to know she's okay."

"Whada you give a shit? The way you tell it, she's the one set it up. I'm glad she did Betso. But he's got her now and that's her tough luck. Fuck her where she breaths. It's the only way."

"It's *your* only way," I said, watching closely while his face grew sanguine, his thick neck began to pulse and his fists opened and closed in unison. The man had me terrified. But there comes a time with creeps like this when you have to stand up.

I stood up, stuck my finger in Scarlo's face, and promptly lost my voice.

There was nothing wrong with Scarlo's.

"So here's what we do," he said. He made a fist, stuck out his thumb and counted: "Number one. You gimme the money."

The thumb folded abruptly and I wondered what happened to numbers two through five. Either he had never learned to count in school or he never watched Sesame Street.

He was through talking and it wasn't hard to find the take home message. I pressed him anyway. "What happens then?" I said.

He reached out and brushed the wrinkles from my lapels. "You live happily ever after."

"Simple as that," I said.

"That's right. Whats'a matter, you don't want my help? You wanna take on Alfie by yourself?"

"If need be," I said.

"Listen, you asshole. There's only one way outta this for you. That's me. You gimme the scratch, I'll deal with Betso."

"Sure," I said. "You'll deal with Betso. What's your plan, John? To set a meet so you can blow him away?"

He grinned. "And I thought you was stupid."

"I must be," I said. "Because I like your plan. It gets me off the hook and puts you in solid with Adonis. But there's another problem. You may be doing this for his benefit, yet I doubt he'll appreciate it. Might be smart to clear it with him first."

Scarlo's grin cracked into small, ugly pieces. "Don't be a smartass. Hey! Pay good attention, 'cause I ain't gonna say it over. Keep away from Adonis. I see you with him and you're dead. I hear you talked with him, you're dead. You got that?"

"Absolutely."

"Now you're makin' sense," he said. "Okay, let's have it."

"The money," I said.

"The money," he repeated.

"Sorry, John."

He blinked a few times, shook his head once and gazed off at the wall. There was no clue on the wall so he turned his attention back to me. "Say again."

"Simple," I said. "You want to meet Betso. Go ahead. You don't need the money for that. He'll think you've got it and agree to meet. After that it's up to you. I mean, he wasn't getting the money anyway. This way it's safe, and so am I."

"So are *you?*" he said with utter shock.

"Yeah. The way I see it, John, that money's life insurance, you know? You want Betso, and I want the girl and me to stay alive. I'll agree to keep away from Adonis if you agree to stay away from me. That goes for Betso, too. Get him off my back and I'll give you the money. That's my deal. You can break all the bones you want, it won't change it."

I glared at Scarlo with all the contempt I could muster. I was bluffing, of course. I couldn't intimidate him no matter how I glared. No. The real threat was the tacit understanding that if he leaned on me I'd go to Manny Adonis. There was still a good chance Scarlo would go at me anyway. But not while I had the money.

Scarlo made a move like he was going to rip my face off, then checked himself. I could almost see that warped brain of his turning and twisting with rage. I'd won this round but the fight had just begun. He'd be back with whatever it took to bury me.

"All right," he said. "But you get down with Manny and I swear I'll fry you like a steak." He gestured vaguely. "Right in your own fucking oven."

Sally came in with the night's take, a handful of bills tied in rubber bands. Where the hell was Linda Dorsey? It was three a.m. and she hadn't returned. Since Scarlo's angry departure, I'd been calling every ten minutes, hearing nothing but Roxanne's prerecorded message. My guess was that at this very moment the Dorsey sisters were having a family reunion.

"Ten thousand, eight hundred." Sally rippled the cash with her thumb. "Not bad for an absentee owner."

I had a combination safe in my office, a heavy gray Sentry camouflaged inside a walnut cabinet, on top of which sat the VCR and the TV. Normally I'd lock up the weekend receipts for deposit on Monday. This wasn't a normal anything.

Gesturing toward the safe, Sally said, "Well? You gonna take this or what?"

I shook her off. "I don't want it in that safe. Take the money with you. Deposit it Monday."

"Just like that?" she said. "Take it with me, eh? Look, Frank, I don't know what's going down here and I'm not sure I wanna know. You been acting weird since you got back from Atlantic City. I'd like to help you out but what you're asking's dangerous. This neighborhood? At four in the morning?"

"I'll walk you out to the car," I said. "You'll be all right once you're out of here."

She puffed her cheeks and exhaled loudly. "How long is this crap gonna go on, Frankie? I mean, I wanna know should I start looking for a job. You don't look too stable, if you hear what I'm saying."

"I'm fine. Really, Sally."

"Sure. Fine and dandy. First Adonis shows up with half 'a Brooklyn. You throw a hairy fit because some broad you don't even know walks out on you. Then Scarlo storms out like he's got pepper up his ass." She waved the money at me. "Now this. It's too fucking much, Frankie. I mean it."

"All right," I said, resigned. "Leave the money here. Forget the whole thing. You're right, it is dangerous."

"Oh go to hell," she said. "You know I wouldn't leave you. Where would I find a job like this? You're so easy to rob it's not even a challenge. Okay, give me half an hour to clean up and we'll take that moonlight stroll to my car. Who knows, I might get a kiss after all."

I laughed. "Perish the thought."

As Sally walked out, the phone rang. Actually it was the bar phone that rang: I heard it from inside. The light flashed on my desk phone. A moment later, Sally buzzed me.

"It's for you, Frankie."

"Is it Linda?"

"Yeah. Linda with a bass voice. It's a guy name Carmine. You wanna take it?"

"No," I said, "but I will."

There's a hundred different ways to let a caller know you're there. I usually say, "Hello." When I'm pissed off I say, "Yeah."

I said, "Yeah."

"Fontana?" It wasn't Carmine. "It's me."

I'd never known a wiseguy who wasn't paranoid about giving his name on the phone. Mr. Betso was no different.

"Yeah," I said again.

"I wanna see you. Right now."

"It's a long drive to Jersey City."

"I saved you the trip. Be outside in five minutes." He clicked off.

Betso, in Queens? My first response was panic. Grab the gun, take the money, run. And go where? With luck, I'd make the Long Island Expressway. Calm down, I thought, stay cool. If the fat man wanted me dead, he wouldn't call for an appointment.

I left the .45 in the desk drawer, told Sally to hang loose, that I'd be back in a few minutes. She demurred but finally agreed.

"Make it fast," she said. "I'm dead on my feet." (Sally always had a way with words.)

I wasn't outside one minute when a car pulled up, long and sleek. The rear window slid down just far enough for me to hear Betso say, "Get in!"

Fat Alfie had most of the back seat. I found some room and squeezed in beside him. "Go," he told his driver.

We didn't go far, a few blocks, to a vacant lot near the edge of the river. I would have preferred an all night diner. But I wasn't asked.

We parked facing Manhattan, a pretty sight—if you're into it. The lights of the bridge sparkled.

So far, no one had said a word. Without looking back, the driver said, "You want me to shake him down?"

Betso swiveled his bulk in my direction. "How about it, Lover? You carryin'?"

I said, "I thought this was going to be friendly."

He grinned. Even his gums were fat. "He's right, Lou. A friendly chat. Go on, take a walk. Not too far, eh?"

Lou got out and positioned himself a few yards away.

"Guess you're wondering why it took so long," Betso said. "Truth is it took some time to squeeze your friend Carmine." He chuckled. "You oughta see him, Fontana. You know that nose he's always braggin' about? Well, it's on the other side of his face now. Same could happen to you. Not tonight maybe. Or tomorrow. It's something to think about, though."

"Is that why you got me here—to threaten me?"

"I don't know what you paid Jake to double deal," Betso said. "Whatever it was won't be enough when I find him."

"What do you mean, when you find him?"

"You hard'a hearing, scumbag? Least he had the brains to run. You got some balls, pal. Pull a scam like this and go right back to work. You're fulla shit if you think the people from Brooklyn are gonna bail you out. So live it up while you can, pal. But hear this. I know what you walked away with." He paused for effect. "When you turn it over, I wanna see every fucking dollar."

He rolled down the window. "Come on back, Lou."

"That's it?" I said. "All the way from Jersey City for this?"

"Don't stretch your luck, Fontana."

"What about the girl?"

"What about her? What goes for you, goes for her. Tell her I said so."

I stood outside the restaurant for a while and fumed.

It had been a set up from the get-go. Roxanne's sidling up to me in the casino, meeting Carmine, the big game on the twelfth floor that just happened to be taking place at the same time. Bullshit!

Roxanne knew who I was before she ever saw me. Someone had paid her to sucker me. No doubt the influential lover.

I pictured the two of them holed up somewhere, the shock on his face when she broke the news about grabbing the wrong bag. I would love to have seen it. A man with power and influence and a lot of my dirty laundry.

Whoever the guy was, he'd had a fix on me from the start. He knew where I'd be and when I'd be there. It cut the possibilities to a precious few. Adonis was among them, though a remote one. Because scamming the fat man out of big bucks was bound to disrupt their peace. They'd have a sit down. Betso would demand satisfaction and Adonis would laugh in his face. Like throwing a seven, the end result would be a natural: war!

I didn't think Manny Adonis wanted a blow out with Fat Alfie Betso. It was possible, yet if that were true, why use me to start the damn thing? A civilian, for Christ's sake.

I figured I had a day or two before the banana cream pies hit the fan, before Betso got his okay to walk in and bag me. Meanwhile he'd settle for Jake. Maybe he needed the dealer to prove his case. Some case, I thought. Jake was no easy get. If the man wasn't dead by now, he was wishing he was.

I went inside.

Sally was ready to call it a night. That made two of us.

Everyone else had left. The only lights were the red bulbs over the exits. "Check the locks," I told her. "I'll be with you in a minute."

"Hurry up," she said. "It's creepy out here."

I went to my office to pick up the night's take. While I was there I removed the .45 from the desk drawer, checked the clip, released the safety, tucked the gun inside my belt and went to join her.

"You're right," I said. "It is creepy out here."

"You got the receipts?"

"In my pocket. Let's go."

Sally's car was across the street, in front of a bagel store that had gone bust years ago. I would have welcomed its reopening. Especially here, a short block from the East River. On a summer night, at low tide, it could knock a man out. From what I was smelling, it was definitely low tide. How, I wondered, could anything with gills ever live in that?

I waited for Sally to get in the car before giving her the money. Until she closed her door, the interior light was like a beacon. She opened her window and stuck out her hand.

I gave her the money. "Get home safe," I said.

She nodded. "What about you?"

"I'm indestructible."

She smirked. "You and the *Titanic*. See you tomorrow."

She pulled away and I stood there until her back lights were tiny red dots.

Me and the *Titanic*. Right.

I wasn't keen on spending another night in my office. Half the underworld would know where to find me. Then again, so would Linda. In fact, my office was the only place she *could* find me.

I turned on my heels and crossed the street.

The first guy popped out of the shadows like Lamont Cranston. How he'd slipped into the doorway was a piece of work. I couldn't make his face in the dark but the shotgun I recognized. He pressed the barrels against my throat and stepped forward.

"How ya doin'?" said the body/fender man from New Jersey.

I couldn't move my head and, frankly, I had no desire to try.

"Check him out," he said.

Two more materialized. They circled me. One of them patted me down while the other placed a hot hand on my shoulder.

"He's packin'," the frisker said.

"He *was* packin'," said the hot hand as the .45 slid from my waist. "All right. Inside."

It's hard to talk without moving your Adam's Apple. I managed an "okay" and a second later the shotgun was pulled back. "The key's in my pocket," I said.

"Get it."

With a push for encouragement, I dug out the key, opened the door and walked in. Maybe flew in was more like it.

I was shoved so hard that I slid head first across the slick wood floor, colliding with a bar stool that landed on top of me. I was in the process of disentangling when a foot slammed my stomach. There were two veal dinners in there and both made a quick exit. Right onto the foot that had kicked me. It wasn't much of an offense but it was all I could manage at the moment.

"Son of a bitch!" the guy yelled. "Them's brand new shoes. I'm gonna wreck this guy."

"Not yet you ain't."

"Fuck you, Julie! We're gonna work him over anyways, ain't we?"

"Eddie's right," said Number Three.

"Hey, Monk," Julie said to him, "go see who you gotta see, yeah?"

"Fuck you, too," said Monk.

I didn't know which of these three was in charge but I was definitely rooting for Julie.

"Both'a you can fuck me later," Julie said. "Right now we got work to do. Watch the door, Eddie."

"Yeah, yeah, I'll watch the door. But who's gonna pay for these fuckin' shoes?"

Julie, with the shotgun, now turned to Monk, who I recognized as the man driving the Lincoln. "You believe this guy?" he said. "We're catchin' shit from all ends and he's worried about shoes."

"Yeah," Monk said. "Blame him. We wouldn'a caught nuthin' if you'd checked the fuckin' bag in the first place."

"Sue me," Julie said.

Watching these morons in action, I understood how they'd taken the wrong bag. They had to be working for Roxanne. No pro would ever keep them on the payroll. It offered a glimmer of hope. I mean, if I couldn't outsmart these yo-yos, I'd deserve what I got.

I hauled myself to my feet. "Look," I said, "I'll pay him for the shoes."

"Take it!" Eddie called from his lookout.

"Will you shut up?" Julie said. He looked at me. "You're gonna pay for a lot more than shoes, wise guy. I owe you for what happened on the parkway. Two bags. Pretty cute."

"How's the girl?" I said.

"Never mind that," Julie said.

"Smack 'em one, will ya, Julie?"

"Yeah," Monk said. "Whadaya talkin'? Bust his face and get it over with."

"Sure," Julie said. "And what about the money? I mess him up, how's he gonna tell me, eh?" He shook his head in disgust. "Dumb fucks."

I said, "Not like you, right, Julie?"

"Smack 'em, for Chrissakes."

I couldn't see Julie's face too well in the dark yet I knew what he was thinking. There wasn't anything he wanted more at that moment than to smack me around. But somewhere inside his thick skull was a modicum of smarts. There were several ways of getting the money, laying me out wasn't one of them.

I felt good at having doped it out so cleverly, until Julie wheeled and caught the top of my head with the gun stock.

I never saw it. What I did see was a lightning storm, jagged flashes that seared my eyes until they blinded me. I went down.

And stayed down.

12

"Get the door, will ya, Eddie? Hey, Fontana! If you ain't
dead, groan or somethin'."

I groaned. A penlight darted around my eyes.

"See. Told ya."

"Then get him on his feet before he does croak."

Julie picked me up, brushed me off and placed my butt on the
only chair that was still upright. My eyes adjusted to the near
darkness. I blinked several times and gazed at what used to be an
orderly place of business.

It was like the aftermath of a cyclone. The bar was a total mess.
Every shelf, every cabinet devoid of its contents; liquor bottles
strewn about, some open, some broken. Even the register was
upside down.

I let my glance drift casually toward the invisible compartment. The cabinet was empty but the sliding door was closed.

"If you wanted a drink," I said, "you could have asked."

Julie kicked my chair. "No more jokes, all right?"

"Smack 'm," Eddie said.

"What happens now, Julie?" said Monk, who was pacing back and forth in the dark.

If Julie had a plan it was known only to Julie. He rubbed his face as if the stimulation would generate some thoughts. When that didn't work, he said, "Where'd you put it?"

"Forget it, Julie," I said. "You wrecked my place. That's enough for one night."

"How come you're so damn sure of yourself?" he said, genuinely puzzled. "I mean, how come you ain't scared?"

"Who said I wasn't? But you're not here to kill me or I'd be dead already. Look," I said, "I'll make it easy for you. Your boss wants the money. I want the girl. Tell him we'll trade."

"Smack 'm," Eddie said.

"We tried that." Julie shot him a look. "Now shut up and lemme think a minute." He thought for a few seconds. "All right, Fontana. I'll tell him what you said."

"There's something else."

"You're pushing it, pal."

"That's right. I want his word. When this is over, no reprisals."

"I'll tell him," Julie said. "But don't count on it."

"Just tell him. That's all I want."

"That's all, eh?"

"Well," I said, "not really. There is one more thing. An answer."

"Jesus Christ!"

"Will you *smack* that fuckin' guy," Eddie said.

"I don't care what you do," Monk said. "But do somethin'. It's gettin' light out."

I glanced at the front window. The night had turned gray. I

could see the street, a mutt sniffing garbage cans. The lighter it got the worse my place looked. But I ignored that and said, "You haven't heard the question."

"Fuck the question," Monk said.

I shrugged. "That's up to you."

"Why we takin' this shit?" Eddie said.

Julie glared at him. "They want the bread, Eddie. Don't matter how they get it. Now be quiet and lemme deal with this."

"Sure," Eddie griped. "Like before."

Julie eyed me closely in the refracted light. He wasn't happy but he must have sensed a way out for him and his crew. "What's the question?" he said.

"Who you working for? I know Betso didn't send you because I talked to him a little while ago. So who is it?"

"It ain't gonna matter."

"Then tell me."

"Hey, Julie," Eddie said. "You ain't gonna—"

"Can it!" Julie said. "All right, Fontana. But you ain't gonna like it."

"That's my headache."

"We don't know who it is," Julie said. "A friend'a mine called me at Caesar's. Said he had a job. Easy work he said."

"Huh," Monk grunted. "There's a laugh."

"He said you beat Alfie Betso in a card game. That you cheated. He said Betso was a friend'a his and he was doin' him a favor. 'Grab the dealer and bring him in,' he says. He tells me you're makin' a run for it. He gives me a make on your car and tells me to track you down. 'The money's in a blue bag,' he tells me. 'Cept he don't say there's two'a them."

"What about the girl?" I said.

"Yeah," Julie said. "That was an extra. We bring her back, we get a bonus." He shook his head. "Some fuckin' bonus. My nuts are still achin'."

"Who's your contact?"

"Come on, yeah? You had your question."

"Okay," I said. "Tell whoever it is, I'm ready to deal. I'll wait to hear. He knows where to find me."

"Hey, Julie." This from Monk who'd drifted behind the bar. He was still nosing around, getting perilously close to the money. "We're supposed to turn this joint. Not just the bar, the whole fuckin' joint. What about the kitchen?"

Never mind the kitchen, I thought. What about my office? The safe? There was nothing in it, but there could have been. Who the hell hired these guys, anyway?

"What *about* the kitchen?" Julie said. "There's a thousand places he could'a stashed it. We ain't got all day to look. No," he said, "if he's jerkin' our chain we can always come back."

"We ain't comin' back if we're dead, Julie. Jesus Christ, I can't believe this!"

Julie eyed me warily. "He's got a point. You don't deliver, we're all dead. You dig what I'm saying?"

I dug very well what Julie was saying. They were hired to do a job and so far they'd failed miserably. It put the four of us on the same tightrope. One slip and we all went.

Julie backed away, motioned for Monk to come out. "Let's go."

"Do me a favor, will you, Julie? If you see Roxanne, tell her I said to hang in there."

Julie grinned. "Lemme tell you something, Fontana. You're nuts if you think that chick's waiting for you. She ain't no friend'a yours, that's for sure."

Now Eddie piped in. "Tell him what she said, Julie. 'Bout the insurance'n all."

Julie laughed. "That's right. Talk about deals. She's savin' her ass over there. Says if you don't pay over we maybe should torch the joint. Gotta be two, three hundred grand in fire insurance. Either way we get the money. Maybe more, if you know what I mean."

If Julie was trying to shake me up, he was doing a damn good job of it. I didn't like what I was hearing but I couldn't let on.

"What do you expect her to do?" I said. "She's scared. I'd do the same thing in her shoes."

Julie shrugged. "It's your funeral. I just hate to see a guy get pussy whipped."

Pussy whipped. I'd take that with a smile on my face, if that's all there was to it. I knew better. My two day tryst with Roxanne was nothing more than a throw-in, a lure, part of the scheme.

I waited for Julie and his boys to pull out. Then I straightened the bar as best I could. Sally would bellow when she saw the place. But I couldn't worry about Sally. I had a more immediate problem to deal with. Like staying alive.

Adonis had a one and a one, but he couldn't get a two out of it. Neither could I. He knew what had happened and that I was part of it, and my guess was that Fat Alfie had wasted no time putting out the word. I could almost hear him sounding off to Adonis: "This guy, Fontana, he didn't fall off no welcome wagon. He's from *your* backyard, Manny. I don't know if he's on your take but I'm gonna find out. All I can say is, he better not be."

I had to get Manny's ear quick. No easy task. The man was predisposed to listen only to God and a handful of mortals—none of whom included me. I mean, you just didn't go looking for Manny Adonis. He looked for you. And by then it was too late, a *fait accompli.*

What I needed was proof: something, someone to corroborate

what I knew and suspected. It's what Adonis was looking for, too. Why else would he waste his time chitchatting with me.

Okay, so I'd get him proof—that hazel-eyed bitch. She was it.

I left the bar in disarray and rushed to my office. I was worried about Linda. Worried and suspicious. She should have shown hours ago. That she hadn't appeared didn't augur well for either of us.

I tried her sister's place on a long shot. After a few rings Roxanne's answering machine came on. I was about to hang up when I heard a click and a sleepy voice say, "Hello."

"Linda?"

"Yes."

"It's me, Frankie."

"Frankie?"

Talk about lasting impressions. "Fontana!" I said sharply.

"Oh, God. Wait . . . what time is it?"

"Eastern Standard or Rocky Mountain? Come on, Linda, wake up!"

"I fell asleep. Guess I was more tired that I thought. The trip and all. I'm sorry, Frank. Didn't mean to—"

"Never mind that. Have you heard from Roxanne?"

"Yeah. She left a message on the machine. Said a friend was going to see you, that I should stand by."

"That's all?"

"I laid down. Must have dozed off. Did her friend show up?"

"Friends," I said. "Three of them. Same three that picked her up. By now they're giving the boss a message he's not going to like."

"I don't understand," Linda said.

"Look, erase her message and leave one of your own. Say you're staying with me. Nothing else, understand?

"I think so."

"Then grab your stuff and wait for me in the lobby. I'll be there in twenty minutes. I want you with me until this is over."

"All right," she said. "But you don't have to come. I've got a rented car. I'll pick you up in . . . half an hour."

I posted myself in the front alcove, behind the door where I could see Linda pull up. I didn't want her walking around out there. Now that I'd lost my gun, I had no way to protect her or myself.

I waited twenty minutes, then took a break to check the money. No reason. Just to check. The money was there. I thought about moving it but they had already tossed the bar, and the chance of their doing it again seemed remote. I returned to my post.

Ten minutes went by. Time enough to get antsy, to envision more trouble than I was ready to meet. To take my mind off waiting, I watched the sun do battle with some mean looking rain clouds. By the time she arrived the sun had lost its fight.

She pulled up in a white Toyota, saw me behind the door and waved. I waved back. I went out, locked the door and jogged over to meet her.

As I settled in for the short drive to my car—to my surprise—she leaned over and kissed me. I felt like a husband being picked up after the night shift.

"What's that for?" I said.

"I just want you to know that I appreciate what you're doing, Frank."

"Oh," I said, disappointed. I didn't know what I wanted from Linda Dorsey, but it wasn't appreciation.

She was wearing a tan knit sweater that matched her slacks, her blonde hair held back with barrettes. Her face had a freshly scrubbed look but her eyes were still puffy from sleep.

"You look great," I said.

"I look awful. No make-up, no shower. Where we going?"

"My car's around the corner. Stick close to me. I've got a penthouse not far from here."

"You live alone," she said. She sounded pleased.

"More or less."

She gave me what I expected: a puzzled look.

I smiled at her. "Emerald and Mai Ling."

"Oh," she said. "I love cats."

"What is this?" Linda said as I guided her inside the ancient service elevator, a rickety cage whose reliability was at best a fifty-fifty proposition.

It still used a roll handle to control direction. I pushed it forward and we rattled and shook our way skyward. At the top floor we lurched to a stop. Linda clutched her stomach. "Glad I didn't have breakfast. Where you taking me?"

"Penthouse!" I called out. "Last stop!" I smiled. She didn't.

There was enough floor space in the loft for a volleyball game. In one afternoon, Emerald and Mai Ling had managed to fill it. A half dozen easels, drop cloths, palettes, gooey brushes, paint tubes, thinners, and sheets of sketching paper were all over the place. Most apparent though were the many nude portraits of their favorite male model, strewn about like prospective recruiting posters for any number of Eleventh Avenue leather bars.

"Good God!" Linda said, gaping at the mess from the threshold.

"Home sweet home," I said.

"You live . . . here?"

"Usually I straighten up before I go to work. But I wasn't here yesterday. It's my two friends. They make the mess and I get to clean it. It's part of the arrangement."

"Arrangement," Linda said. "Who are these friends?"

"Emerald and Mai Ling."

Linda forced a smile. "Cats."

I grabbed her suitcase. "Follow me, I'll show you where I live."

With mincing steps, we picked our way across the floor, around the debris. Behind me, Linda was saying, "You actually live here. My God!"

"Here it is," I said, drawing the curtain to my modest quarters.

She took a tentative step forward, peered in. "Quaint," she said. "I can see why you sleep in the office. Is there a shower somewhere?"

"All the comforts," I said.

I gave her the nickel tour, about all it was worth. She wasn't impressed. We finished it in the kitchen area. Linda gawked at an antique bag from Burger King. "I wish you could see what I left to come here. That's quite an apartment my sister lives in."

"I'm sure it is," I said. "And her boyfriend pays for it, huh?"

"That's the least he can do. Is there any coffee around here?"

"Sure. Grab a stool, if you can find one."

I put a pot on the stove. While it brewed, I broached a subject I knew would be trouble.

"I have to know who the guy is, Linda. I'm not sure but I think he's behind all this. I think your sister knows it. I think she's with him right now."

"That's crazy!" Linda nearly shouted. "She's in trouble. I told you that."

"It's only crazy if you buy her story about Betso."

"Wait a minute," she said. "Are you saying my sister lied to me?"

"Why? It's never happened before?"

"Yes, but—"

"I talked to Betso. He called me last night. It's not your sister he wants. It's me. Actually it's the money he wants. If he nails me in the process, all the better."

It seemed Linda had a habit of rubbing her forehead when she was troubled. She was rubbing it pretty good when she said, "I don't understand."

"Think about it. Suppose her boyfriend had this scheme to cheat a high-roller named Betso. He rigs the poker game he knows Betso plays in every week. Pays a mechanic to bottom-deal the guy out of three hundred grand. The boyfriend can't be in the game because it's too risky. Fact is he must have known Betso would catch on. He just doesn't care. He doesn't care because he's got himself a sucker. A simpleton. A guy lured into that game to take the consequences."

I leaned over and looked into Linda's eyes. "You getting the picture?"

I gave her some time to fill it in for herself. She seemed deeply troubled. And for good reason. In the foreground of that picture was a young woman from Yonkers who looked a lot like her. Her sibling, Rose Ann.

I sighed. "She had help from a guy named Carmine. But she knew what was going on."

"I can't believe that," Linda said.

"You can't? Or you won't? Look, she's in love with this guy. Only she knows why and how deeply. But I'm guessing it's a one sided proposition. I've been in deals like that before and I know what it does to a person. It's not healthy, you know?"

Linda lowered her eyes; a little misty, a little sad.

"You're right," she said. "It isn't healthy. Hasn't been from the start. I tried to tell her she was throwing herself away, wasting her life. But she wouldn't listen."

"When?" I said.

"When? What do you mean?"

"Was it recently?"

She hesitated. "No."

"So when? Last week? Last month?"

Annoyed, she said, "I don't know. Awhile ago."

"Like last night you mean. Or this morning. You're holding out on me. If you want my help, you have to level with me. Tell me. You talked to her today, didn't you?"

She closed her eyes and lifted her face toward the ceiling. "Oh God, I hate this. I'm no good at it."

I went over to her, touched her arm. "It's all right."

"You see right through me," she whispered. "I told her you would." She looked up at me. "I'm sorry, Frank. I had to lie about it."

"Forget it," I said. "I've got a brother. He's a pain in the ass, too. But if he was in trouble, I'd do more than lie for him."

"You're right about everything. She was sent to get you into that game. I swear, I didn't know until last night."

"She called you."

"Yes. I almost died when she told me about it. That son of a bitch. He's got her so turned around, she doesn't know what she's doing anymore. It wasn't Betso who beat her up. It was him. When she didn't bring him the money he was furious. Blamed her for the mistake. He's threatened her. If he doesn't get what he wants, he'll. . . . She's terrified, Frank. So am I, if you want the truth. These people are despicable."

"Where was she when she called?"

"She wouldn't say."

"What's his name?"

"I don't know."

I swore under my breath. The coffeemaker coughed.

"I've asked her. She's never told me. 'What you don't know won't hurt you.' That's what she says."

"She's probably right. But I have to find out who he is. It's our only chance of getting her out of this. Ourselves, too."

"What can I do?" she said. "Anything at all."

I still wasn't sure if she was jerking me around. I wanted to believe her. But that was the problem.

"The name game," I said. "I'll mention some. Stop me if you hear one you know. Johnny Scarlo."

"No." No hesitation.

"Petrone—Sid, Nick." She shook her head. "Manny Adonis."

"No."

"Julie, Monk, Eddie."

"It's no use. She's never mentioned any names."

"Think," I said. "She must have told you something about the guy."

She rubbed her forehead. "He's a heavy gambler. But that's no surprise. Every man she's ever been with was a heavy gambler."

"That only covers about nine tenths of my clientele."

The coffee began to perk. So did my mind. Heavy gambler, I thought. Show me a heavy gambler and I'll show you a guy in debt up to his colon.

I gave Linda a cup and poured the coffee. It was hot in the loft but she shivered and wrapped both hands around the cup for warmth. She was scared, plenty scared. If I could've had it my way, I'd have sent her back to Denver. But she'd never leave and I wasn't about to suggest it. There was just too much at stake. Like her sister's life. And mine.

She sipped the coffee while I stared at her. Linda and Roxanne—sisters. It was hard to believe.

She glanced at me from over the cup. "You're staring at me."

I nodded. "It's what I do with beautiful women."

"What else do you do?"

"Make mistakes."

"Don't talk that way," she said. "I know what you're thinking. I'm not lying to you. I swear I'm not."

I waved it off. "Still want that shower?"

"More than ever."

"I'll get some towels. I've got a few calls to make anyway."

"What's going to happen, Frank?"

"Well, first you turn on the tap. Step in, get wet, soap up, then rinse."

"Please," she said.

I sighed. "One step at a time. I've got to find out where she is. No ideas, huh?"

"I'm afraid not."

I nodded.

I went around the divider into my room, fished a few towels and a bathrobe from the closet and came back. "One thing about showers," I said. "They're hard to take with your clothes on. You can change inside."

She took the robe. I put the towels on the counter and waited for her to change. She did, quick.

I love the way women look in men's bathrobes. Especially mine. This one, a knee length terrycloth, whose belt I'd lost years ago, reached Linda's calves.

Holding it closed with both hands she padded quickly toward the shower. She'd pinned her hair up in the back. A few loose strands of gold dangled seductively to her shoulders. My ex-wife used to walk around like this all the time: One of those memories I could do nicely without.

I waited till she turned on the water, then went to my room,

checked a phone number and dialed an old pal of mine. I didn't
think he'd be in at six in the morning but I tried anyway.

"Lieutenant Grimm," I told the desk sergeant.

"He's not here."

"I have to reach him right away," I said.

"Who is this?"

"A friend of his. Name's Frank Fontana. Look, it's important.
Can you reach him somewhere?"

"Probably."

"Then try, will you? Tell him I have to talk with him."

"What about?"

"Just tell him," I said.

"All right." He sounded bored. "I'll give him the message.
Does he have your number?"

"Grimm's had my number for some time," I said. "But take it
just in case."

I laid down on the bed while I waited for Grimm to get back to
me. It wouldn't take long.

Grimm was one of those guys who walked around in a per-
petual state of discontent. He was a black man, an honest cop,
and he hated the mob and all those associated with it. I wasn't
exactly, but selling them booze was close enough.

One night, shortly after Fontana's had first opened, Grimm
popped in for a look-see. He took one look at my clientele, and
pulled me aside. "You're an asshole, Fontana. I thought you
learned your lesson. This place . . ." He shook his head dejec-
tedly. "What you got here is a hangout for degenerates."

"What would you have me do, Lieutenant? Screen every guy
who comes in?"

"No," Grimm said. "I'll do that."

For several weeks I viewed every new face with suspicion,

walking around with my nose in the air, sniffing for badges. But the wiseguys had far keener senses. Grimm's men would barely set themselves on a bar stool when every finger in the joint began to point. Eventually, Grimm switched to sporadic harassment, coming in with a few apes, hanging around just long enough to disrupt the flow of business, then leaving. Futile, of course. But no less a pain in the ass.

The phone rang. I picked it up.

"What the hell do you want?" No hello, no how-are-you. It's a bitch when you have to get help from guys like this.

"I want protection," I said.

If nothing else, I'd made Grimm's day. He laughed so hard he began to choke. When he finally settled himself, he said, "What is this? Dial-a-joke?"

"Don't fool around, Grimm. This is serious."

"It always is. With you, anyway. What'sa matter? Kitchen too hot for you?"

"You might say that."

"Then get the hell out!"

"You want to hear this, or what?"

"Go 'head, while I'm still in a good mood."

"They're leaning on me. If I don't pay they'll torch my place."

"I'm Organized Crime," he said. "What you want is Arson."

"What I want is help."

"Call the National Guard."

"Organized Crime, you said. Who do you think's behind this?"

He waited a moment. I knew what he was thinking. A little squeeze play, the quid pro quo of the hungry cop. I was ready for him.

"You want me to guess or you gonna tell me?" he said.

"Will you help?"

"Maybe. I mean what's in it for me? I want names, Fontana."

"Wish I'd known," I said. "I would've asked for a business card. All I saw was a shotgun and three ugly faces."

"Sounds scary."

"It was. It is."

"Well," he said, yawning, "let me know how you make out."

"Hold it!" I said. "All right, you got me. But only first names, that's all I heard. Julie, Monk and Eddie."

"Monchinetti? That's one wop I don't know."

"*Not* Monchinetti. Monk *and* Eddie."

"So long, Frankie."

"Alfie Betso," I piped quickly.

"Fat Alfie?" That got him. "From Jersey City?"

"If you say so."

"They said Betso sent them? They told you that?" He sounded excited. A big bust, decorations, promotion. Whatever turns you on, Grimm.

"Absolutely," I said. "How about it? You in this or not?"

"Absolutely," he said. "Tell me more."

I gave him what was known to the Fontana brothers as quasi-bullshit. A modified version of the truth. Enough to entice without spoiling the game. I told him I'd met Betso a while ago in Atlantic City. At the tables, I said. Strictly innocent: two gamblers comparing notes.

"I never should have mentioned the restaurant," I said. "Guess I bragged too much. Made it sound like the Four Seasons."

Grimm wasn't snagged yet. The hook was set but he hadn't swallowed it.

"Something's off," he said. "Betso's big in Jersey, but to make a move in the boroughs he'd need an okay. I don't know, Fontana. I think you're strokin' my tits."

I said, "I'm just telling you what happened, what I heard. Why would I make it up?"

"Don't know." He paused. "But I mean to find out. When did they come in?"

"This morning, right after close. Scared the shit out of me."

"Like before, eh? What's your story, man? I mean what the hell are you, a frustrated Al Capone? When are you gonna learn that you can't play with these people? The more you kiss their ass the more they get off on it. Lucky for you there's no law against aiding and abetting the criminal image. That's one thing you're very good at. Well, let me tell you something. You lucked out with Candy Gizzo because I was there to save your ass. Now it's Betso. Maybe this time I'll pass—let him bring you down. It would serve you right, you know?"

"You finished?" I said. "Lecture over?"

"No, Goddamnit! But you won't learn till it's too late, if it isn't already." He skipped a beat, then said, "All right. I'll put your place under surveillance until I sort this out."

"That's good enough. Thanks."

"Don't thank me. Thank the taxpayers. I'll be in touch."

He hung up.

Grimm hadn't told me anything I hadn't already heard—from Grimm. Still, he meant well and for the most part he was right. Maybe I *was* a frustrated gangster.

I was whipped. I must have been. When a woman gets into bed with me, I usually know it. Linda had crawled in beside me and I wasn't aware of it until a pair of familiar voices jarred me from a sound sleep.

"Will you look at this?"

"Aaaah, how sweet."

Linda bolted upright. The robe fell open for a moment and that woke me up real quick. "What? Who . . ."

I pulled her down. "Relax."

She fought me. "Relax? Who are these two?"

I raised myself onto my elbows. "Linda Dorsey, meet Emerald and Mai Ling, President and Chairwoman of Loft Wreckers Anonymous."

"Oh my God," Linda said.

"Be cool, honey," Emerald said. "We won't tell."

Linda frowned at me. "Cats?"

"Yeah, well . . ."

"You could call us that," Mai Ling said.

"I've been called worse," piped Emerald and high-fived Mai-Ling.

It took a while to sort things out. For the most part I kept quiet, allowing my loftmates to explain in detail the pertinent facts I'd kept from Linda. She took it well and in time even laughed about it, warming to the girls' ingratiating ways.

An hour later, after I'd showered and shaved, I joined the ladies in the kitchen for an elegant breakfast, compliments of Mai Ling and Dunkin' Donuts.

"What'll it be, Frankie?" asked Mai. "We've got jelly, blueberry, and lemon."

"Two eggs over."

"Get real," Emerald said.

"Never mind. Just coffee."

Linda poured. "I'm very impressed with their work," she said.

"Thank you." Emerald bowed. "But wait till you see our model."

"In the flesh," added Mai.

"Not again," I groaned.

We chatted a while. At ten o'clock I pulled Linda aside, told her I had to go out, that I'd be gone for several hours and she absolutely, positively should not leave the premises. She balked.

"I want to go with you."

"Not until we find your sister. Just stay by the phone in case they call. And for God's sake, don't give your name."

She was about to protest when a sudden commotion broke it off. Emerald and Mai Ling, their shrill cries proclaiming the arrival of Alfonso, Mr. Beefcake, replete with body oil. It was time to split.

Bookies, when you want them, are easier to find than cops. They keep regular hours and their hangouts are well known on the street. One of Bobby Chubbs' favorite hangouts was a dingy bar called the Anchor Inn.

I'd known Bobby Chubbs for years, from my early days when I tended bar at the Skyview Lounge. At the Skyview, Bobby and I had this arrangement: I'd shave his tabs and he'd pad my tips. For a little extra I would turn him on to the high rollers and point out the dead wood. It worked out well for both of us.

Of course the arrangement ended when I opened Fontana's. I allowed him to take his action at the bar but I'd never asked for anything in return. Until now.

The Anchor Inn was on Metropolitan Avenue, about twenty-five minutes from my loft. It was one of those long, narrow gin mills. A neighborhood joint with an old wooden floor and a ceiling of corrugated tin. I found Bobby in a booth in the back. He seemed deep in thought, staring down the neck of a soda bottle.

"A deuce for your thoughts," I said. "In the fifth at Belmont."

He looked up at me and blinked. "I don't believe it," Bobby said in his weird, high-pitched voice. Everything about Chubbs was big and burly except his vocal chords. He looked like a tuba and spoke like a flute.

I stuck out my hand. "How you doing, Chubbs?"

"Big Frank." How the hell are ya?"

"Fair to midline."

He giggled. "Fair to midline, I gotta remember that." He paused. "So what's up? You got a hot one, or what?"

"Not today," I said. "I need a favor, Bobby."

"Name it," he said.

"You may not like it."

"I'm listening."

"It's about Johnny Scarlo," I said.

"That douche bag." He drank his soda, smacked his lips and said, "What about him?"

"You take his action, don't you?"

"Yeah," Chubbs said. "Though I wish to Christ I wasn't."

"I understand, Chubbs. Don't worry, no one's going to know we talked."

"That ain't what I mean," he said. "He's into me for some major bucks. Been jerkin' me around for days now. Keeps yakkin' that he's close to a score. But I don't know. I think he's fartin' at the moon. What's going on? He owe you, too?"

"Yeah," I said. "He owes me."

"Well, don't hold your breath, kid. I like you but I come first, you know?"

"No sweat. Just wanted to know where I stand."

"You're in the crapper. The two of us. Serves me right. It's too much to lose, even for him."

"How much?" I said.

"It's yacht money, Frankie. A trip around the world with a two week layover at Monte Carlo. Next time you see me, kick me in the ass, will you?"

"We'll kick each other, Chubbs." I got up. "Oh, one more thing. You ever see him with his girlfriend?"

Bobby sucked air through his teeth. "Which one? Guy's got more broads than I got aggravation."

"This one you'd remember. Auburn hair. Hazel eyes with some green thrown in. Likes to gamble."

"Could be," Bobby said. "Seen him once in a joint on East 78th Street. Dorado's. Had this chick on his arm, could be the one. She gave me a bet. Hundred to win on a fifty to one shot."

"Dorado's on East 78th Street. You're sure about that?"

"Dorado's, yeah. Ask for Joe P., he's a friend'a mine."

"Thanks a lot, Chubbs. I appreciate it."

"Anytime, partner."

"The fifty to one shot," I said. "Did it win?"

Bobby smiled and gave me a wink.

13

"Where we going?" Linda said, as we rumbled over the 59th Street Bridge, racing the Roosevelt Island cable tram into Manhattan.

"Dorado's," I said. "It's a restaurant."

"You should've told me. I would've changed my clothes."

She was wearing jeans and a clingy scoopneck blouse. "You look fine," I said. "Besides, we're not going there to eat."

What I was doing was building a case against Scarlo, facts I'd present to Manny Adonis when the time came. Fact number one: Scarlo was the one who sent me to Bally's. Fact two: No one else knew I was there. Fact three: Scarlo knew Betso's gambling habits, his propensity to lose. Fact four: Scarlo was in hock up to his ears.

Those I maybe could prove. What I didn't have was the fifth

and most important. The rock that would bury Johnny Scarlo and get me off the hook: Roxanne Ducharme.

Except for Scarlo, no one knew more about what was going down here than Roxanne. Somehow I had to get her and Manny together, get her to talk, get him to listen.

All well and peachy. But I had to find her first. Find her and take her with me. Sure thing, Frankie. Never mind the goons who'd be holding her. One look at you and they'll turn her right over. Absolutely.

I started looking for Dorado's; I cruised East 78th Street. Linda seemed edgy, kept looking around.

"This looks familiar," she said. She pointed to a swanky high rise. "Hey! That's Rose Ann's apartment house."

"Yeah," I said. "And there's Dorado's."

It was Sunday, which meant there were places to park. I found a spot near the restaurant and pulled in.

"I'll be back in a minute," I said. "Wait here. Keep your eyes open and don't get out."

"What's going on?" Linda said. "Is my sister in there?" She fumbled with the door handle. I grabbed her arm, pulled her back.

"Take it easy," I said.

She struggled. "Lemme go!"

"She's not in there. Relax, will you?"

She slumped in the seat.

"Look," I said, "I'm going in to ask a few questions. She and her boyfriend have been coming here. I wanna check it out."

I guess it was bound to happen. She put her face in her hands and began to cry.

"It's all right," I said. I took her in my arms. She buried her head in my chest, and sobbed.

"I . . . I'm so worried, Frank. If anything happens—"

"She's fine," I said. "Believe me, nothing's going to happen."

"I feel so . . . scared for her."

"I know. Just trust me, all right? We'll find her."

She lifted her face, mascara running down her cheeks. Her eyes were moist and so were her lips. They looked soft.

I fished in my pocket. "Here's a hanky," I said. "I'll be right back."

The stuff inside Dorado's had to cost some heavy bucks. Lots of marble and glass; wild chandeliers and low slung divans. They had signs around that bragged about Sunday brunch. Today's feature was shad roe with bacon—$19.95, and all the Mimosas you could drink. From the size of the crowd, they could have used a few more signs.

The bar man lit up when he saw me coming. He was wearing a scarlet vest and a plaid bow tie with matching cummerbund. All dressed up and nothing to do.

I grabbed a bar stool and he set me up with a cocktail napkin. "Nice day," he said, nodding his head toward the window. It was cloudy out. He shrugged and smiled. "Well, at least there's no rain."

I ordered a Virgin Mary. He poured the juice from a can and placed the glass in front of me.

"I'm looking for Joe P.," I said.

His face dropped. "Who wants him?"

"I do. I'm a friend of Bobby Chubbs."

"*I'm* Joe P.," he said. "What can I do for ya?" He didn't sound friendly.

"We're looking for somebody."

"Ain't we all," he said. "But I'll bite. Who is it?"

"Johnny Scarlo."

His jaw went slack. It stayed that way for a moment. Then he closed it.

"Well?" I said.

"You work for Chubbs? You a collector? I was you, I'd find a new job."

"I know he comes in here," I said. "Him and his lady. You know . . ." I snapped my fingers . . . "what's her name . . ."

"I don't know," he said. "It's your pitch. Look, I don't know *who* you are. You say you're a friend'a Bobby's. You put two bucks on the bar and ask me questions you got no right to ask. Be a nice guy—take a walk."

I took fifty bucks from my wallet, placed the bills on the bar. "That make it better?"

"You could triple that and it wouldn't matter. I like Chubbs, but not that much."

I picked up my glass and took a sip. "Okay," I said. "Forget Scarlo. It's the lady I'm looking for. Name's Roxanne."

He grinned. "Now you remember, eh? Must be the tomato juice, jogs the memory. Yeah, I know Rox. Comes in here once in awhile."

"When's the last time you saw her?"

He looked down at the fifty bucks. I nodded.

"Last night," he said.

"Last night? You sure?"

He shrugged.

"Was she alone?"

"No. Two guys." He shook his head. "But not *your* man."

"Names?"

He laughed. "Tweedle Dee and Tweedle Dum." He snatched the money and walked away.

I left Joe P. counting to fifty and went out to get Linda. Her eyes were dry and fixed on the front door. When she saw me she seemed relieved. I motioned her out.

"What happened?" she said, excited.

"Later," I said. "Come on, I wanna check her apartment. You've got the keys, right?"

"Yes, but—"

I took Linda's hand and led her up East 78th Street. She had questions. So did I. One in particular. It was the first thing I said when she unlocked the door. "Why didn't you tell me you saw her last night?"

"Rose Ann? I *didn't* see her. Honest!"

"Honest, huh? You're up here having a nap while she's down the block having dinner? Come off it!"

"I swear," she said. "I never saw Rose Ann. I told you, she called."

"I know what you said."

"I'm not lying," she pleaded. "Don't make me say it again. Please, if you know something, tell me."

I told her what I'd learned from Joe P.

Her eyes went wide. "Then she's all right?"

"I don't know what she is. But if she's being held against her will, they wouldn't take her out to eat. Especially here, in her own neighborhood."

Linda shot me a quizzical look. "What are you trying to say?"

"It's obvious, isn't it?"

"Not to me it isn't. She wouldn't get me here from Denver if she wasn't in trouble."

"Well something doesn't fit. She's all over town, for Christ's sake. Dinner with the boys—explain that one!"

"I can't," she said. "But I'm sure there's an answer."

"Oh, there's an answer, all right. Trouble is, we're not gonna like it."

While Linda pondered, I glanced around her sister's apartment. It was everything I thought it would be—airy and plush. Twenty-one stories above the street, picture windows and an open terrace for catching the rays. Not a bad pay back.

"I'm going to look around," I said.

"Let me help," Linda said. "I have to do *something*."

I stared deeply into those opaque eyes and tried to read behind them. She appeared sincere but I couldn't tell for sure. Too many years with the wrong woman maybe.

I said, "Will you make some coffee? I'd ask you to help but I'm not sure what I'm looking for."

"Is that the reason?" she said. "Or don't you trust me?"

I had accused her of lying and she was hurt. I could see it in her face. Maybe I *was* too suspicious, judging one sister by the other. For all I knew, Roxanne was using the two of us. In which case, Linda was in for a heavy fall. If I was smart, I'd be there to catch her.

I moved closer and reached out for her. She pulled away. "No," she said. "You're not sure and neither am I."

"Try to understand," I said. "I'm only going by what I see."

"What would you like me to do?" she said.

I had to keep telling myself that this was Linda, not Roxanne. That regardless of what I was used to, there *were* decent people around.

I said, "You're right.

Her frown melted away and she gave a little smile. It brought out a dimple I hadn't noticed before.

"All right," she said. "I'll make the coffee. Black, no sugar. Right?"

"Any way you do it," I said, "it's fine with me."

While Linda searched the kitchen for a coffee pot, I searched the bedroom for anything that might lead us to Roxanne. What I found was an indirect route.

The coffee was waiting for me but I didn't need it. I'd taken something that belonged to Roxanne. It was all the stimulant I wanted.

"Come on," I said to Linda. "I'm taking you back to the loft."

"You found something?"

I shook my head.

If Linda knew I was lying, she didn't let on. She was more concerned about what I planned doing while she cooled her heels.

"All right," she said reluctantly. "I'll wait for you. But tell me where you're going at least."

"I'm going to Brooklyn," I said. "Something wrong with that?"

14

I'd seen the Greenpoint Social Club a few times from the outside and always wondered what went on behind those black painted windows. I pictured a smoky room with a dozen or so guys sitting at folding tables, reading the sports page, playing pinochle, killing time between killings. It was a helluva way to spend your life. Then so was sitting at a desk cranking out reports for some corporate type who barely knew your name.

I parked across the street and down the block from the club where I wouldn't be observed. It was three o'clock on a Sunday afternoon but you'd never know it by the number of guys going in and out. Most of them were strangers to me. After about forty minutes my man showed his face. He stepped out, squinted up at the sky, then looked around.

I slid quickly beneath the dash, praying he hadn't seen me, that he wouldn't walk in my direction. How long would it take

Scarlo to reach me? Twenty seconds? I gave him a full minute, then rose slowly, peered over the wheel down the block. No sign of him. Do it now, Fontana! And pray to God he doesn't return while you're in there.

The front door was made of wood, all wood with no windows. I tried the knob but it didn't turn. No surprise. I was about to knock when the door opened.

"Whadaya want?" This from a man who could have doubled for a wrecking ball. About five-five and just as wide.

"I'm a friend of Mr. Adonis," I said.

"So?"

"I'd like to see him."

"You and a hundred like you. So-long, *friend.*"

"Wait," I said. "He told me to come here."

What I got was a look that fell somewhere between disbelief and acrimony. At least I think it was a look. It was hard to tell through his scrunched up eyes. "What's you'a name?" he said.

I shook my head.

He backed away and gestured me in. I love the way these characters communicate.

"Stand here," he said and lumbered across the floor like a two-legged rhino with hemmorhoids.

The club was everything I'd imagined. A single room with knotty pine walls sporting sepia photos of the Brooklyn Dodgers, circa '55. Ashtrays piled high atop a half dozen unoccupied poker tables; the fragrances of yesteryears cigars. An overstuffed couch on the near side. A tall coffee urn on a long table. In the far corner a portable TV in front of which sat a pair of aspiring Dillingers.

They were watching the zany antics of Lou Costello. No laughs, no smiles. Nothing more than catatonic stares disturbed by my nervous cough and the shifting of weight from one foot to the other.

They rolled their heads casually in my direction. If I posed a threat, they didn't show it. Thank God.

"Over here," said the wrecking ball.

Over here was a doorway that led to an office. I crossed the room and went in.

Now this was an office. Not like mine. No cots in here. No VCRs. Or used furniture from Goodwill. This was the genuine article, the high-priced spread on a piece of white bread, culture shock compared to what I'd just walked through. Thick rug, mahogany walls, padded chairs. An executive suite from which any chief would be proud to reign.

Manny Adonis rose imperiously from the depths of a high-backed, red leather chair. He placed his hands on the broad expanse of a sleek, cherrywood desk, leaned forward to balance his weight, and said, "The answer is no."

"I haven't asked for anything."

"No." He adjusted the cuffs of his Jermyn Street shirt. "But you will. Why else would you be here?"

"You don't understand," I said.

He raised an eyebrow. "Is that so? Then let me ask *you* a question. Would you be talking to me now if you weren't scared to death and desperate for help?"

"No," I said. "I wouldn't."

"So you see, Fontana? I do understand. Perfectly. Besides, I already told you, there's nothing I can do. You shouldn't have come here. There's a lot at stake and I can't have you messing things up."

"I came here to help you," I said.

He eyed me for a moment, then chuckled softly. "That's a switch. Guess today's my lucky day, huh? Yours, too, maybe."

He checked his watch, a gold field mottled with diamonds. "All right," he said. "I've got a few minutes. Take a seat and let's hear it."

I'd been around guys like Manny Adonis long enough to know that if they respect anything it's candor. I took a chair in front of his desk, settled in and said, "Your problem isn't Betso. And it certainly isn't me. It's right here in your own outfit."

I didn't wait for his response. I gave him what I'd lifted from Roxanne's bedroom. It was a five-by-seven glossy with a hand-written date on the back. A month old photo taken at Bally's Grand.

He scoped it out for a moment. No expression of surprise. Nothing. I waited. Five seconds, ten. A frigging lifetime. "It's Scarlo," I said.

Manny's head jerked. "I'm not so old I can't see. Who's the babe with him?"

"That's what I wanna talk about."

He tossed the photo on the desk. "Don't play it simple. Just tell me what you want."

"What I want is your word. If I can prove what I say, am I okay?"

"I told you to work this out on your own."

"That's impossible and you know it."

"Don't tell me what I know," he bristled. "It's not polite."

"I'm sorry. It's just that . . . well, look what I'm up against. If Betso doesn't nail me, Scarlo will. He knows I'm the only one can hang him. He warned me to stay away from you. Threatened to fry me if I came here. Why would he do that if he didn't know?"

Inching forward in his chair, Adonis regarded me with sudden interest. A welcome change.

"He talked to you after I came in?"

"The same night. He told me he's after Betso. Said he was

doing it for you. But it's bullshit. It's the money he wants. I wasn't sure until this morning."

"What happened this morning?"

"I found out he's in hock with the bookies. Some heavy debt. He's playing them for time, promising to settle up after he scores a big deal he's working on. I don't have to tell you where it's coming from."

"No," Adonis said. "You don't have to tell me. Forget it, Fontana. Forget it the way you forgot everything else I said the other night. I told you how things are with Betso and me."

"But I can prove it was Scarlo."

"That's the whole point," Adonis said. "I don't want you to."

I started to speak but nothing came out. "I don't get it."

"Naturally. Because you don't listen. What do you think Betso will do if he finds out it was my own man who fleeced him? Jesus Christ. Johnny Scarlo is my number one. You're bright enough, do I have to spell it out for you?"

"You're killing me, Mr. Adonis. You really are."

"I don't know, you look pretty healthy to me."

"For how long? If you tie my hands, I'm a dead man."

"No one's tying your hands. And stop whining!"

"I'll grovel if I have to. Jesus Christ. I thought you'd *want* to know."

"Who says I don't?"

"Yeah, but—"

"But, but," he said. "You say you can prove something. What I get is a snapshot." He lifted his chin at the photo. "You expect me to ice Scarlo on that?"

"No," I said. "But if I can back what I say, will you help me?"

"I don't know. Maybe." He steepled his hands beneath his chin. "What do you have in mind?"

134

"The girl in the picture," I said. "She'll confirm everything I say."

"Why should I believe *her?*"

"She's the one who got me into that game. Scarlo sent her to snag me."

He waved his hands in front of his face. "Hold it, hold it. You told me she wasn't involved. You said it was this Carmine Genovese. Make up your mind, which is it?"

"Neither—. I mean they're both involved. But they didn't brain the thing. Scarlo did. Hell, I'd never even heard of Betso until that night. Listen. He sends me to Bally's. Meanwhile his girlfriend's waiting for me—"

"And now you're suddenly ready to sell her out, huh? Not like the other night. 'No girl, no money'—that's what you said."

"I'm still saying it."

"You're a joker, you are. You want me to take Scarlo out so you can have his girl. All's fair in love and war?"

"That's not it, not at all. There's nothing between us. A couple of nights and no attachments. She was doing what she had to do."

"For Scarlo's sake," Adonis said.

"Exactly."

"All right," he said. "Let's suppose that what you're saying is true. She's crazy about the guy, do anything for him. Now you come along, Frankie Fontana, the white knight with a handful of menus instead of a lance. Two nights with you and—" he snapped his fingers— "just like that she turns him over. Is that what your sellin'?" He shook his head. "I've never met this babe but I know plenty like her. They're—whataya call them—like groupies. A flashy guy like Scarlo makes a play, pays a few bills, they're hooked for life. I'll admit you're better looking than he is. But I don't see her giving up this *gumba* for someone like you."

"She's not giving him up. It's the other way around. He's going to waste her when this is over."

"Is that right?"

"He has to," I said. "She's the only one can bring him down. Her and me."

Adonis went silent. He swiveled his chair a half turn and gazed vacantly at the near wall. I followed his gaze to a series of lamanated scrolls. There was one from a volunteer ambulance association, a men's club and the Citizens For a More Beautiful Greenpoint. The man was a model citizen.

He swung back to me. "You willing to face him with this? Head to head?"

"With you there?"

He nodded.

"Absolutely."

"Good," he said. He ripped a sheet off a scratch pad, scribbled a number and held it out. "Call this number. Let me know where I can reach you. I'll check around. Everything tracks, I'll get back to you. Meanwhile, you and the broad stay low. I don't want her to see him until the time comes. What's the matter? You look sick."

"That's just it," I said. "I don't know where she is."

15

"**D**umb bastard! Stupid son of a bitch!"

Manny's echo was still bouncing off the walls when the door to his office flew open. The wrecking ball was breathing heavy, panting from the short run, blocking the exit in what he thought was a call to arms. "You want me, boss?"

"Get out!" Manny shouted.

The man shrugged and backed away.

I waited for Manny's face to regain its natural color. Talk about volatile.

"Let me explain," I said.

He was still hot. "Explain what? We're not playing poker here, Fontana. You don't bluff and you don't bullshit. Not me, you don't. I'm thinking you've got the girl in your hip pocket and you don't even know where she is. I'll tell you where she is. On cloud nine, playing a golden harp."

"I don't think so," I said.

"You don't think so. Listen, that broad was dead before Scarlo showed his face."

"Mr. Adonis, please, listen to me. The girl's alive. At least she was last night."

"You saw her?"

"No."

"You talked to her."

"Not exactly. I mean not directly. She spoke to someone I know."

"Who's that, God? She talked to God and God talked to you?"

"I can't explain it now," I said. "But it's true. Scarlo's holding her somewhere. I intend to find her. When I do, I'll bring her in."

"Just like that, huh? What are you going to do? Say, 'Please, Johnny, give me your girlfriend so I can bring her to Manny?' You and what army? Not mine."

"Just give me one day," I said. "Twenty-four hours. Keep Betso off my back for that long and I promise I'll do what I say."

For a long moment we just sat there eyeballing each other, exchanging messages. From me, desperation. From Adonis, skepticism.

Finally, he said, "You're a bit confused, aren't you? Your problem isn't Betso. It's Johnny."

"I'll deal with Scarlo," I said. "He doesn't have you behind him. He's in this on his own so he has to be careful what he does. But Betso." I shook my head. "He'll come to you when he's ready. When that happens, you'll have no choice. Just hold him off for a while. That's all I ask."

"Then what?"

"He's after me now because he thinks I cheated him. I can't say that I blame him. But if he knows it wasn't me and I return his money, would he still want me?"

138

Adonis leaned forward, cuff links glinting. "Are you dense, or what? Here, watch my lips. It's not you Betso wants. It's me. Just your being here is a liability. You give him Scarlo and you're giving him me." He sat back. "How do I explain that my top man's a liar and a cheat? I don't even want to, for Christ's sake. It's demeaning."

"Not necessarily," I said quickly. "It's not your fault you've got a rotten apple in your outfit. So you throw it out. Hell, you'd be doing him a favor. Yourself, too."

What I was asking was close to impossible. Scarlo had ripped off his main rival—an unsanctioned scam the combine would never condone. The only way to make it right was for Manny to admit to Betso that he'd been taken by his own man. Do-able for someone else, perhaps. But Manny Adonis? I didn't think so.

He cocked his head and gazed off into mid space. The wheels were turning. He looked at me. "Tell me straight. Can you do what you say?"

"I can do it."

"All right. We'll dance for a while. You've got the number. Call when you get the girl. I don't know how you're going to do it. That's your headache. I'll pass the word you weren't here. That's all I'm gonna do."

"That's enough," I said.

Adonis smiled. "You're pretty sure of yourself."

"I have to be."

"Lemme tell you something." He leaned closer. "There's only one man who can reason with Scarlo. That's me. You try to finesse him, you'll be singing lead soprano at High Mass."

I hurried back to Queens and made a quick stop at the restaurant, where I suffered the indignity of Sally Plunk's verbal onslaught.

Her bar had been ravaged and she would damn well ravage someone in return. Me.

"That's it!" she ranted. "That's fucking it! I'm off today. But do I stay home like a normal person? No. I come in 'cause I'm worried you're all broken up."

"That's sweet of you, Sal."

"Sweet *this*," she shouted, grabbing her ass with both hands. "Look at this place."

"It looks fine."

"Sure. Sure it does. I broke my nuts for two hours and it still looks like shit. What kind of joint are you running here?"

Sally's tirade had sent the rest of the staff scurrying for cover. When I yelled I got dirty looks; to Sally they listened, or hid.

I said, "Some overripe boozer wanted an after-hours drink. I refused, we tussled. I straightened up as best I could."

She blew steam for a while but finally calmed herself. "I don't believe a word of this," she said. "This was more than a tussle, Frankie. I mean the whole damn bar was upside down. I've got a right to know. Are we in trouble, or what?"

"We're okay."

"Oh yeah? Then who's Julie, huh? He's been ringing the phone off the wall. Every ten minutes: Where's Fontana, where's Fontana? The guy's no salesman, I'll tell you that."

"What did he say?"

"I told you. 'Where's Fontana?' 'Not here.' 'Tell him Julie called.' Click. Stick around, he's overdue."

As if on signal, the phone rang. We traded looks. "See what I mean?"

I picked it up. "Fontana's."

"I know that," Julie said. "Is it you?"

"It's me."

"Where the hell you been?"

"Church," I said.

"Yeah. Okay, listen up. I gave your message. We're ready to deal. Tonight, ten o'clock. Northwest corner, Thirty-fourth and Broadway."

"Manhattan?"

"Yeah. Bring the bag."

"You bringing the girl?"

"Just bring the bag. You'll see her." He hung up.

Sure, Julie, I'll bring the bag. Bupkis, that's what I'll bring.

While Sally waited for the update she'd never get, I called the loft. Linda answered.

"How's it going?" I said.

"Fine. The girls have been great. They're characters, all right. But you have to like them."

"They still there?"

"They're getting ready to leave. Alfonso's getting dressed."

"Must be tough on him," I said.

"He's okay." Pause. "I've been worried. I didn't know what to do so I tried calling Rose Ann again. No message. You coming home?"

Coming home. I liked that.

"Be there in a few minutes," I said. "I'll bring us dinner. Give them a kiss for me, will you? Alfonso, too. He'll dig it more if he knows it's from me."

Within the hour I was back at the loft, setting tableware on a flakeboard counter top. An early dinner. Lasagna with meatballs, its tangy aroma lost amid the heady smell of paint and turpentine.

Linda looked great. Fresh make-up, blonde hair caressing her shoulders. She dabbed her lips with a paper napkin. "Well?"

"It's set for tonight," I said, chewing.

"What? What's set for tonight? Come on, Frank, it's no time for lockjaw."

"I'm eating."

She frowned.

"All right," I said, "here it is. At ten o'clock I go to Thirty-fourth and Broadway. I'll meet some guys. We negotiate. I get your sister, they get the money." I popped a meatball, chewed and swallowed. "Should have brought wine," I said.

"Forget the wine. What else?"

"That's it. An even swap."

She lowered her fork. "I may live in Denver, Frankie, but I think New York. You're not kidding me. It's not that easy. You know what they'll do when they get that money. Now come on, what's the catch?"

"Wish I had wine."

"If you go tonight, I'll never see you again."

"That bother you?"

She nodded. "I've been thinking about what I said. About trust."

"So have I."

"This thing tonight, it's a trap. They'll keep the money and kill you both. It's no good."

I winked at her. "It's no good if they get the money. That's why I'm not bringing it. Look," I said, "I worked something out today. Roxanne's the key. There's a guy I know wants a talk with her. She tells the truth, backs my story, well, we should be okay. It means ratting out her boyfriend. I'm worried she won't. That's where you come in, Linda. You'll have to convince her. It's our one shot."

"Convincing her isn't the problem. She'll listen to me if I have to strangle her. Getting her free, that's the problem. How?"

"Not sure," I said. "Have to see what happens, where it goes."

142

"That's great. Wonderful! No plan. Walk in, grab Rose Ann, walk out. Merry Christmas, Frankie."

"Eat your dinner," I said.

"I can't eat. You, you're putting it away like it's your last meal." She shook her head, hair swaying. "Maybe it is. I can't figure you out."

I yawned. "All this scheming knocks me out. Always has. What I need's a bed, recharge the old generator."

With an incredulous gaze from those hazel eyes, she said, "How can you sleep at a time like this?"

I gave her a half smile. "Who said anything about sleep?"

"Oh, God. Oh, my God."

It wasn't easy to hear Linda with my ears buzzing. Her legs were wrapped over mine, thighs pressing me in. I'd known from the time she undressed, she wasn't like Roxanne. But what can I say? Some things you just have to test.

Linda's moves were like Roxanne's. Similar, but more intense—Roxanne played at love. For Linda, it was serious business. Nothing desperate, no hang ups or guilt. Making love was an act only in the physical sense. She wanted me and wasn't afraid to show it.

I wanted her, too. But I held back.

She pulled me up. "No more. My God, no more."

She held me tightly, squeezing her legs with a rolling motion that fell neatly into mine. If there was a world outside I didn't know it. Didn't care to. I was deep into the great escape and ten o'clock was an eon away.

I hadn't smoked a cigarette in years. But it never changes. I always want one after sex. Especially this kind.

"What time is it?" I said, Linda beside me, sweat against sweat, the smell of passion and perfume thick in the air.

She covered my mouth. With a hand first, then lips. A long, serious kiss, soft, moist. "Don't talk," she whispered. "Not yet."

We let the mood carry us, playing out that peaceful easy feeling while time ticked away. After awhile, she stirred. "I'm thinking about coming back to New York," she said.

I placed my hand over her mouth. "Don't talk," I said. "Not yet."

16

It hadn't occurred to me that the northwest corner of 34th and Broadway was the eastern corner of Macy's. It seemed like an odd place for a meet. On a different night it would have been. But this was Sunday, retailers closed, tourists uptown, and most sane New Yorkers at home, gearing up for the new week.

The sidewalk was deserted. I found a spot, parked and waited, eyeing the pavement for unfriendlies. I was looking for three men. Only one showed up.

It seemed odd to see Julie without his sidekicks. Stranger yet was the way he shuffled along, head down, preoccupied, in no particular hurry. He approached my car, leaned forward and peered in through the passenger side. I opened the door. He checked the back seat and got in next to me.

"I don't see it," he said.

The guy seemed dejected. Like he knew I wouldn't bring the money and wasn't surprised.

"Where's Monch'n etti?" I said, trying a joke.

He shook his head slowly, fished a cigarette and lit up. On the exhale, he said, "I had the feeling, you know? From the start. Eddie and Monk, they warned me not to take this job. Bush leaguers playin' the majors. How was I supposed to know?"

"Know what, Julie?"

"Heavy hitters," he said. "Alla' them. What the fuck did I know?"

"What heavy hitters? You mean Johnny Scarlo?"

"Don't know any Scarlo. Shit, ain't Betso enough?"

"Ever think about changing sides?"

He gave me a vacant look, then took a drag and turned away.

"We can help each other," I said. "Throw in with me. They can't have more than two or three guys watching her. We're four, with Eddie and Monk."

"Forget Eddie and Monk. They're makin' tracks. But you can't outrun these guys. Nobody can." He looked at me. "You're my last shot. Don't suppose you brought the money."

"Fraid not."

He nodded, took another drag. "Figures. You're one oily son of a bitch, ya know that? Well, you'll be joinin' us. I don't know, coulda' been easy. Shoulda' been. You're lookin' to make trades when any guy in his right mind woulda' coughed up and run like hell. I'd 've let you go, if you gave me the money. Fuckin' hard ass. All the guys in the world, I get a hard ass." He shook his head, resigned. "Come on, let's go."

I tried to draw Julie out but he wouldn't talk. His fate had been decided and he had accepted it. With grunts and vague gestures he steered me downtown, then uptown to West 37th Street, heart of the garment district. By nine a.m. there would be curb to curb commerce: trucks blocking traffic, runners by the hundreds hauling giant rolls of fabric on long dollies and pushing racks of clothes up and down the street, making wise cracks to pretty girls through a haze of car fumes and pot. Ten p.m. Sunday it was a concrete cemetery.

I followed Julie inside a gloomy, worn out building, along a narrow corridor and into a small self-service elevator. He punched a button and up we went.

"How many men?" I asked.

"Three, if you count me."

"Should I?"

"Lemme alone, will ya?"

Again I followed Julie. This time through a door that accessed a huge expanse of floor space — a storage area, from the look of it. Floor to ceiling fabric, walls of material, roll upon roll forming a maze that required a guide to negotiate.

We clomped along an old wooden floor, a few lefts, a few rights and out of the fabric forest.

I was facing an office, more like a booth — half panel, half glass. Roxanne was sitting in a folding chair under a flickering light, staring blankly at a pebbled window over a gray-metal desk. She looked unhurt. Also unnatural. Like someone had drugged her, propped her up and she'd been there ever since.

I looked for the someone but didn't see him. What I saw were file cabinets and mountains of paper alongside, the wide soapy stuff used by designers to create patterns. The door was open. Julie slid to one side and motioned me to go in.

One thing for sure, Roxanne wasn't drugged.

She heard my approach and leaped to her feet. "You're okay," she crooned, running toward me. "Thank God, you're okay." She threw herself into my arms, hugging me, kissing my face in a hundred places. Welcome home.

I held her at arms length. I wanted to look her over, check for bumps and bruises. She looked fine, unscathed in fresh slacks and a pullover.

"You changed your clothes," I said. "War is hell, isn't it, Rose Ann?"

She seemed flustered, wriggled her fingers at me and was about to speak up when I heard a familiar voice. "Frankie F. How the hell you been? Still servin' that shit you call food?"

"How you doing, Nick? Hello, Sid."

Apparently, Scarlo was through playing with second stringers. It was late in the game and Julie's crew had failed to score. So he'd pulled them and replaced them with his starters, a pair of hitters who liked to play dirty.

Stepping forward as one, the Petrones pointed their guns. "Where's the money?" Nick said. He looked to Julie for an answer. But Julie still wasn't talking. The guy was pitiful.

I wasn't feeling too brave myself at that moment. But I wasn't ready to pack it in.

With no gun and no money, about all I could do was blow hot air at them, buy time until I caught a break. I started blowing. "You got a pen? I'll write a check."

Roxanne was all kinds of nervous, flexing her knees, jiggling around like she hadn't peed in a week. "What're you saying, Frankie? You can't talk like that. Look at their—"

"I've seen guns before."

"Yeah, except—"

"You want out of here, or not?"

"Sure, but—"

"You'd better choose sides, Rox. And do it fast. I know the whole story. So no games, okay?"

"There's no need for this, Frankie," she said. "Believe me, it's okay."

"Is that right?" I turned to Nick and Sid. "How about it, guys? Everything cool? Copacetic?"

"Shut the fuck up!" Nick said. "I don't like you, Fontana."

"Me neither," piped Sid. "You're foulin' up the works here. Makin' it difficult. You call the shot and you back out. What the fuck?"

"Yeah," Nick said. "You got the money or don'tcha?"

"I have it. But look, why don't we just drive over to Jersey City and give it to Betso. Cut out the middle man, you know?"

"You're askin' for it, man. I mean you're beggin'."

We stood there for several long moments, Julie sullen, Roxanne bouncing around, the Petrones completely befuddled. They weren't used to this kind of bravado in the face of their arsenal. Neither was I.

Nick broke the impasse. "So what is it? You wanna deal, we deal. Back out and you're dead. Make up your mind."

"Money for the girl. Right?"

"Hey, prick with ears, you want it in writing? What is it?"

"We'll have to get it," I said. "Me, Julie, and Rox. I'll give it to him, he'll bring it back."

Sid and Nick gaped at each other the way brothers do when they're trading information without talking.

Nick said, "You want us to wait here while you take a ride. That the story?"

I nodded. He was huffing.

"That's so fuckin' lame I can't even laugh. No. What we do is this. Me and Sid, you and her, we all four take the ride."

"What about me?" Julie said.

"You? You're goin' south when the time's right. Now beat it."

"Yeah," said brother Sid. "And don't call us for no fuckin' reference."

Julie accepted his short-term reprieve the way he'd accepted his ultimate fate. He gulped loudly, blinked once and dropped back, disappearing in the maze of fabric.

We listened to the fading sound of Julie's footsteps. When the fire exit door slammed, Nick said two words: "We go!"

We were going, but where? I should have listened to Linda, devised a plan and stuck with it. Have to see where it goes, I'd told her. So far, where it was going was down the tubes. One tube, anyway. An elevator shaft down which the four of us descended. The last place I wanted to take these guys was the restaurant. Lieut. Grimm had said he'd watch the place but I wasn't sure he would. Even so, the Petrones would smell him a block away. So what's to do? A tour of Queens? Brooklyn? Forget it!

They kept us in front of them, prodding our backs with gun barrels, herding us toward the street.

It could have been the company but the street seemed darker than it did before. A few cars were randomly parked, no sign of life.

"There," Nick Petrone said—a four-door Cadillac in front of a loading bin across the street, about twenty yards away and too close for me to come up with anything bright. Where the hell was that plan? Do I spin around and swing? Clip one Petrone while the other shoots? Would Roxanne help? Was God watching any of this?

So far, Roxanne and I were oh-for-one in street fights. Having lost to Julie and his band of misfits, what chance did we have against Nick and Sid? Little to none, I figured. Especially out in the open, no witnesses, plenty of room for gun play.

In the car, maybe. Nick driving, Sid in the rear seat, covering us. We grapple, two against one, Nick no threat with his hands full of steering wheel.

Nick gave the keys to Roxanne. "You drive!"

Great. One against two.

Sid opened the rear door while Nick stood by. "Get in," Nick said.

Spin and swing. Don't think, just do it!

But I couldn't move. I couldn't get in the car and I definitely couldn't swing. My guts had dropped to my feet and I was mired where I stood. I knew I had to fight but I just wasn't ready. I needed cause. And fear alone wasn't getting it.

Then something happened. Lights flooded over us, a car came to life. We looked back at the blinding headlamps. Who was it? Not that I cared.

Nick grabbed Roxanne and held her. Sid shoved me aside. He raised his gun as the car lurched forward, heading right toward us. He fired twice. The car swerved but kept coming. If I needed cause, I was staring at it.

I lowered my shoulder and threw myself at Sid. He stumbled halfway across the street. I went after him, bowling him over before he could turn the gun on me.

His head struck tarmac with a dull thud. The average head would have cracked. Not Sid's. I took aim and kicked. Sid howled, a high shriek in perfect harmony with brother Nick who was in Roxanne's vice-like grip. She had him good.

The car was barreling dead on. I didn't think it would stop. It hugged the left side of the street and clipped the door right off Nick's car.

"Look out!" I yelled, jumping to one side as the door flew in the air, missing my head by inches.

The car skidded and stopped. A white Toyota.

"Come on!" Linda shouted through the open window. "Get in!"

"Go on, go on!" I urged Roxanne. "Let him go, for Chrissake!"

She hesitated like she wasn't sure it was okay to turn Nick

loose. But Nick was white in the face and brother Sid was still rolling around. I rushed over to Roxanne, yanked her arm and pulled her away.

"It's Linda," I said. "Hurry up, get in!"

She gave Nick one final, defiant look, then jumped in the car. I dove in after her. "Hit it!"

Linda floored the pedal. The motor raced like hell. We didn't move. The car was in neutral.

"Fontana!" Nick squealed. "You're dead. You're fuckin' *dead.*"

Linda dropped it in gear. The tires spun in place for a second, then caught with a screech. After a mighty lurch, we fishtailed down the block, Roxanne shouting, "Yeah, yeah!" like some kind of overdressed cheerleader at the Indy 500. "We showed 'em, Frankie! We got 'em, didn't we?"

I looked back. The Petrones were hurt and hobbled, but they were on their feet, helping each other, moving gamely for their car.

"Not yet," I said. "Not quite."

17

"Are you okay?" Linda said. She had to turn to see her sister who had jumped in the back.

"I'm fine, Lin. God, it's good to see you. You believe this? I'll tell you, I was never so glad in my life."

"And I was never so scared in all my life," Linda said. Her eyes were now fixed on the road she had to crane her neck to see. The damaged left fender was a snarling mass of metal jutting upward. "When that man shot at me . . . I didn't know what to do. I knew Frank was coming for you so I followed him. When he went inside with that man, I was frantic. Then you came out and—"

"Pardon me," I said, slumped next to her. "I may be wrong but I think we're being chased."

Roxanne groaned. "Not again."

Linda hadn't noticed the Petrones in their modified three-door Caddie. She was too preoccupied with conversation as we headed uptown on 6th Avenue, cruising at a comfy thirty-five, stopping for lights no less.

"I don't see anyone," she said, shifting her glance to the rearview mirror, casual like, as if all our problems were behind us. They were behind us, all right. And closing fast.

"Talk to her, will you, Rox? I don't think she understands. Back there," I said. "Those are the bad guys. They have guns and when they're close enough, they'll use them. Now step on it — straight to 59th Street and *don't* stop for lights. If you see the cops, blow your horn. They'll think you're nuts and pull us over."

"Lin, that was beautiful," Roxanne said. "What you did."

"*Later*," I yelled, "for Chrissake. Talk later. They're coming up!"

Roxanne took a quick look. She flushed and began pounding her fist on the headrest. "He's right. Hurry up, Lin. Faster, faster!"

The first shot hit the back window and came out the front. How it missed us, I don't know. But it shattered the windshield and caused enough panic to send us caroming off a parked car. We bounced, richocheted, swiped a moving cab and listened to Linda scream.

I'd watched a hundred movies, a thousand car chases, not once did I believe it could ever happen on a city street. Much less 6th Avenue? Avenue of the Friggin' Americas, five lanes across.

"What should I do?" Linda cried, fighting the wheel as if the Petrones were somewhere under the hood.

The second shot k.o.'d the side mirror. Linda screamed, Roxanne too. We had to squint against the rush of air whistling in through the vacant windshield, bits of safety glass all over us.

"Keep going," I urged. "But watch the crossings."

Traffic was light but this was Manhattan. Light traffic here was a motorcade in Akron. Any intersection could mean instant demolition.

We cleared 39th Street without trouble, then 40th. I looked back hoping to see Nick's Caddie impaled on a crosstown bus. But he had cleared it with ease and was moving up.

On our right was Bryant Park, 41st Street to our left. Next stop, 42nd Street. I watched the traffic light go from green to yellow. *Walk* became *Don't Walk*. And the open space before us began to close with two-way traffic.

With no place to go, Linda hit the brake.

"Don't stop!" I shouted. "Go right, go right!"

"Oh, God," cried Linda, and promptly turned left.

The first guy saw us coming, hooked to the right and raced by. The guy behind him stopped short, took a rear hit and veered over. On the other side, both lanes gave way with a blast of horns and bellowing curses. Nick tried to follow our path, but too late. East and west were converging, every hole blocked.

There was that sickening hollow thud, an instant's silence, then glass breaking.

"Go, go!" I yelled.

For once Linda listened. She was too psyched not to. Somehow the heavily damaged Toyota ate up the road in swift, healthy chunks.

"I don't see them," Roxanne said, peering back through the bullet hole in the rear window. The 42nd Street sin strip shot by, all the lights a blur.

"Which way?" Linda cried.

The Hudson River was rapidly approaching, the Jersey cliffs looming across the water. "Take the next left," I said.

I waited for a right but she made the proper turn and we headed downtown. After a few more turns I told her to slow up.

"Where we going?"

"Underground," I said. "Pull over."

She found a spot on a dark street. I reached over, shut down the motor and killed the lights.

"What now?" Linda said.

"We wait."

We sat there in the darkness for several long moments. Linda, down in her seat, eyes closed, flinched a few times as if watching a mental replay. I kept my eyes peeled for any sign of the Petrones while, in the back, Roxanne grew fidgety.

"I suppose I oughta thank you," she said.

I smiled at her. "We're partners, aren't we?"

She said, "Yeah," but it sounded feeble. "You should've brought the money, Frankie."

"Your half? Or mine?"

"All right, I deserved that. But you don't know what you're doing."

"It's the other way around," I said. "You're the one doesn't know. You want out of this or don't you?"

"It's not that easy."

"Is that a fact? Well, thank you very much. I'm enlightened."

"Leave her alone, Frank." Linda was waking up to what was going on. "She's been through hell."

"Gee, that's rough."

"It *has* been," Roxanne whined. "You don't know."

"No," I said, "but I can guess. Dinner for three at Dorado's?"

"How'd you know about that?"

"Never mind. Your boyfriend's not a very nice fellow, leaving you alone with the Petrones."

"It's not his fault. It's Sid and Nick, they're the ones. They can't stand us being together so they make trouble. It's been that way from the start."

"Is that why you fought them? Or you just enjoy breaking balls?"

She bit her lower lip and looked down. "Not now, Frankie. Please."

"Not *now?*" I said. "Not now? Listen to me, lady. I've got about fourteen hours to put this straight. After that, I've got every hammerhead in New York and Jersey coming down on me. You got me into this. The least you can do is cooperate."

"It's raining," Linda said.

I turned to the windshield, looking for spots on the glass. The only spots were those on my pants. The rain was coming in. Perfect.

"We'll have to go back for my car," I said, "and get out of this wreck before we drown."

"Go back? Are you crazy?"

"Sid and Nick have their own problems," I said. "Besides, they'll never expect us to go back for my car." It took some doing but I finally convinced them we'd be okay.

We took the subway to 34th Street and Herald Square, then walked the last couple of blocks. Then we picked up my wheels on 37th Street.

"Where you taking us?" Roxanne said as I fired up the engine.

"I told you. Underground."

"I've *been* underground," she protested. "I'm tired of it."

Twenty minutes with Roxanne and she was already being difficult. This wasn't going to be exactly fun.

"You'll like this place," I said. "It's got all the comforts of home."

There must be a hundred or so motels in Queens and Brooklyn, motels of every quality and design. Out in Sheepshead Bay was an adult playpen called the Briny Breezes. It was once my ex's special haunt.

The Briny was a good forty minute drive from the restaurant. I didn't like being that far from my investment and the hidden money. However, keeping Roxanne away from the action seemed more important than playing watchdog over something I couldn't protect anyway.

It took an hour to get there from Manhattan. An hour of excited chatter from Linda, and griping and sulking from Roxanne. She wanted her clothes, make up. A toilet. She was nauseous from the ride, achy, pre-menstrual. She was scared, angry, disgusted. She wanted Scarlo.

"This is crazy," she said as I turned into a parking slot in front of the Briny, the neon sign flashing *Adult Motel . . . Adult Motel.* "He won't hurt us if he gets the money."

Linda bristled. "He's already hurt you. He slapped you around, didn't he?"

Roxanne poo-pooed this with a waving hand. "Oh come on, Lin."

"Come on my ass! You were terrified, Rose Ann. And that was no act."

"That was before I knew."

"Knew what?" I said.

She took a few seconds to come up with an answer. "Before I knew you'd help. I was afraid you'd run away, Frankie. That's why I called Linda. I needed someone to stay close . . . to the money I mean. That's a lotta bread and, . . . Johnny's in serious trouble."

"What are *we* in," I said, "a state of eternal bliss?"

"I mean it," she insisted. "He's borrowed money and he can't pay it back. It's a short-term thing but you know how it is with those people."

"Yeah," I said, "I know how it is. Lose money you don't have, then go out and steal what you owe. Nice."

"It's more than that," she said. "Don't ask me what, because I can't say. Frank, I love him. And when you love someone you help. Doesn't matter if he's right or wrong. You help."

I looked at Linda. "You believe this?"

"No," Linda snapped, "I don't." She turned to her sibling and began lecturing. "You listen to me, Rose Ann. You've been chasing bums your whole life. Now they're chasing *you*. We're lucky to be alive, for God's sake. Where does it end? Don't you care?"

Petulant, Roxanne said, "I care."

"Then show it!"

"Here, here," I cheered.

Roxanne glared at me. "I wouldn't talk if I was you. You have a stake in this, too. Several hundred thousand bucks."

"Wait a minute," I said.

"Be quiet!" Linda said. "I'll deal with this. I've been dealing with it for years." She turned back to her sister. "This man, Scarlo—look me in the eye and tell me he loves you."

"He loves me," Roxanne said, her eyes downcast.

"Look at me!"

Rose Ann Dorsey, alias Roxanne Ducharme, lifted her pretty face, wiped the tears from her cheeks, and said again, "He loves me."

It was so pitiful I was embarrassed for her. I mean here's a woman, flaming hair, full of fight and fire, hard as steel, reduced to whimpering. All in the name of love. Man, how I empathized.

I turned away. Linda stayed on her.

"You wish!" she uttered sardonically. "If you believed what you're saying, I'd know it. I can see right through you. You know I can. So no more bullshit. No more mooning over some hoodlum who'd sooner kill us all than take you to bed one more time. Now smarten up. Do what's right for once."

I was about to applaud, until I remembered James. How many times had he lectured me on similar subjects, brother to brother, offering help and sound advice? How many times had I listened?

I was beginning to think it was too late for Roxanne. She didn't care that we were trying to save her. Her sister had dodged bullets for her, and I had made a *meshuggena* pact that had reduced my life expectancy to hours. None of it mattered. She was under a spell, Svengalied by a social misft. The lady was in love and I knew damn well she'd bolt at the first opportunity.

We went inside the Briny Breezes.

The last time I had made love to my ex-wife was in room 133. I asked for it and it was available. The room hadn't changed: waterbed, mirrors, sunken plastic tub, blue movies on cable. About all they didn't have was room service, unless you counted the concierge, who doubled as bouncer, a heavyweight who patroled the halls responding to cries of frenzied masochists. Instant eviction and forget the refund.

But no coffee and donuts. No late snacks from an all night cafeteria. At the Briny you got what you brought. I could have checked in with a wooly sheep on a leash and not drawn a second glance. As perversions go, even two gorgeous look-alikes were little more than exotic.

Roxanne checked the room like a building inspector on the take, her nose turned up at everything she saw. "What the hell are we doing in this dive?"

"Staying alive," I said. "Sit down and relax."

She leaned over the bed and turned her face up toward the overhead mirror. "What is this? If I didn't know my sister, I'd swear you got us here for an orgy."

"Don't be tacky," Linda said.

"Why? Don't you think he's capable?" She gave me a lascivious look and said, "Believe me, Lin, the man's very capable."

Linda caught my eye, flushed, and turned away. Roxanne picked it up.

"Oh," she said, "so that's how it is. Never too busy, huh, Frankie?"

"Knock it off," I said.

"I want a drink."

"There's water in the bathroom."

She grumbled and threw herself across the bed. The waterbed rocked and rolled. So did Roxanne. "Jesus Christ," she said. "I'm getting sea sick."

"Look," I said, "we're going to be here for a while. Don't make it difficult, all right?"

"You're the one who's difficult."

"How do you figure?"

She tried propping herself on an elbow. The bed swayed. She fell back and found herself staring up at the mirror. Distracted by what she saw, she fluffed her curls and said, "I can straighten this whole thing out in five minutes. Just give me the phone."

I looked at Linda who'd taken the chair by the window, the phone beside her on a walnut table. I said, "If she goes for that phone, break her fingers."

"Don't you worry," said Linda.

We just looked at each other while the clock ticked away the time I didn't have. I needed Roxanne to come around. She had to turn on Scarlo. I gave it one more try.

"Let me ask you something, Roxanne. If you knew Scarlo was planning to off us all, what would you do?"

"He wouldn't do that."

"He's notched people before, you know."

"That's what *you* say."

"Oh, I forgot. Only the Petrones clip anybody. Scarlo's their boss, for Chrissake. How do you think he got there? By going to night school? That's not General Motors he works for. A guy fucks up, they don't demote him. They snuff him."

"I know that," she said testily.

"Then you must know he's desperate. He'll do anything to get his hands on that money—sweet talk your ass from here to China if he has to. Once he has it, you gotta know he'll leave no witnesses."

Roxanne closed her eyes, hugged herself and turned away. I knew how she felt. The truth's a bitch when you've been living on love and lies for so long. Linda got up, went to the bed and sat down on the edge. She placed a hand on her sister's shoulder and stroked her hair.

"I know it's hard," Linda said. "But you have to listen to him."

Roxanne shook her head several times. "I know, I know. I . . . he's no good. I just can't believe he'd do it. Even while Sid and Nick were holding me, I couldn't believe it." She gazed up at her sister, eyes moist. "What's wrong with me, Lin? Why do I keep doing this? I'd never let him hurt you, though, you know that."

"I know," Linda nodded.

"So do I," I said. "But how do you expect to stop him?"

She knew she couldn't. All she could do was close her eyes and let the tears run. "I'm tired," she said. "I wanna sleep."

I motioned to Linda. When she was close enough, I whispered, "Let her sleep. Are you hungry?"

"Who can eat."

"We're going to be here all night. Let me go out and get something. If she wakes up, keep her quiet."

"I wish you wouldn't go," she said.

"Don't worry, you'll be okay."

Now it was Linda's eyes filling up. She hugged me tightly, gave me a kiss and said, "Hurry back."

Actually, food was the last thing in the world I wanted. Some coffee maybe, three blacks to go—heavy caffeine for the all night vigil. What I really wanted was a telephone. The phone in the room wouldn't do. I couldn't risk spooking the girls. Not with Manny Adonis on the line.

There was a public phone in the lobby. But it was too close to the omnipresent scrutiny of a desk man whose job it was to prevent the very thing I was about to arrange: trouble on the premises.

When he heard me coming, he raised his face from the pages of a D-cup magazine and gave me the eye like he expected a challenge.

I eased his mind. "Any place to get coffee around here?"

"Holiday Inn," he mumbled.

I've always wondered what Ma Bell had in mind when she did away with phone booths, those neat little enclosures with seats and bifold doors that allowed a person the privacy of conversation without freezing his ass in the winter or drowning in the rain. These days it was kiosks—or half a kiosk. You stick your head in a box and scream over traffic while your legs and feet get splashed.

I found a kiosk about eight blocks away, jumped out of the car and stood there in the rain as I dialed the number Adonis had given me. An unsociable gent with a gravel voice answered the call. "Seven, eight, five," he said, reciting the last three digits.

I knew better than to ask for Manny by name. So I gave the following message: "Tell the man I've got the girl and she's ready to talk. We're at the Briny Breezes, Sheepshead Bay. You got it?"

"Got it."

Quick and easy. If only it were.

With my back soaking wet and my feet in a puddle, I dropped another quarter and called Sally. "It's me," I said.

"Hurray," she said.

"What's happening?"

"We're still in business, if that's what you mean."

"Come on, Sal, get serious."

"Whadaya want me to say? It's quiet."

"Good. Close it up and go home."

"That's just what I had in mind."

"Any sign of the law?"

"We got robbers but no cops. Why?"

"Nothing," I said. "Forget it."

"That's easy for you to say."

I got in my car and began searching for an all night diner. As I drove around I wondered about Grimm. Sally hadn't seen him but that didn't mean he wasn't there somewhere, staked out, protecting my interests even though he hated the idea.

The whole trip, including the calls and the search for coffee, took fifty minutes. I figured to find Roxanne asleep and Linda watching television.

What I found was disquieting.

18

The room was so packed with men I thought the girls had sold tickets. Scarlo, the Petrones, and two other guys I'd seen around. They grabbed me, knocked the coffee out of my hands, and threw me against the wall.

"I didn't get enough sugar, huh?"

Roxanne and Linda cowered in a corner. They looked okay but frightened. Which made it unanimous.

Scarlo moved toward me. A menacing presence anywhere, he seemed more so in the confines of the crowded room.

"Had'a do it, didn't ya? I told you to stay away from the guy, but you had'a do it."

"What are you talking about?"

"Shut up!"

I looked at Roxanne. "You called him?"

Scarlo's hand shot out so quickly I never saw it. But I felt it sure enough. A stinging blow that caught my cheek. I wasn't back ten seconds and already I was cut and bleeding.

"*You* called," he said. "Twenty minutes ago. Lucky for me I was right there. 'Message for the boss? Give it to me, I'll take it.' But all right. What's done is done. I'll straighten it out later." He didn't look that confident, I thought. "I don't care what you told him 'cause he ain't gonna help you anyway. Nobody's gonna help you, not no more. What's gonna happen is this: you're takin' a trip. You, Sid and Nick. You're gonna get that money and hand it over. Me and the boys are gonna wait here, catch a laugh or two with the Ditso sisters. Ain't that right, girls?"

"Oh, Johnny," Roxanne cried. "Don't do this. Please."

He glared at Roxanne. They locked eyes but she couldn't hold it. She lowered her face and backed herself deeper into the corner. Then Scarlo turned his glare on the Petrones.

"I'm surrounded by fuck-ups," he said. "First her, then you two. Christ, what a crew."

"We'll make it up, John," Nick said.

"How? You gonna do Manny? You couldn't handle *them*. Two broads and a putz like him. Yeah, you'll make it up. Tomorrow."

"We'll get the bread," Sid told him. "Just like you want."

Scarlo looked at me. "How about that, Fontana? Will they get it?"

I dabbed my cut cheek with a hanky, checked the blood and said, "What happens later?"

"There ain't gonna be no later for you."

"What about them?"

"That depends," he said. "Do the right thing, I'll cut 'em loose. Get cute and I'll just cut 'em. You hear what I'm sayin'?"

"Yeah," I said.

Liking what he heard, Scarlo pursed his lips and moved his neck in and out like a hungry chicken. Then he patted my face a few times, real friendly. "That's good, Frankie. I mean you're makin' sense now, you know?"

"Yeah," I said.

"Hey, look, it ain't my fault. I know it's a bitch but that's how it goes sometimes. A plan goes wrong, you gotta improvise. I got nothin' against you, 'cept you got a big mouth." He shrugged. "I guess I was you, I'd do the same."

He turned to Nick Petrone. "Do him quick, Nickie."

"Sure. If he plays it right."

"He'll play it right. Won't you, Frankie?"

It's a helluva thing when you have to act polite to a guy who's out to kill you.

"I'll play it right," I said. "You have my word."

He laughed. "I got your word and I got your balls. But don't worry, Frank. You'll close your eyes, hear a pop, and it's all over. Better guys'n you went down that road."

"And they'll be plenty more to follow," I said. "Right, John?"

Scarlo squinted at me. "Like me, for instance?"

"What do *you* think? Manny knows all about it. The whole scam. Waste me and you'll prove everything I've told him."

"That's what *you* say. It's your word against mine. And by morning you ain't gonna be talkin' much."

"It doesn't have to come to this," I said, trying desperately not to sound desperate. "You can't use that money anymore. You come up with it and they're going to know. Let me go to Betso. I'll keep you out of it. I'll give him his money and take my chances."

"Funny you should say that," he said. "I was thinking the same thing. 'Cept it won't be you giving it over. The way I figure is this—you're right. I can't use it no more. Not for what I wanted. It's too bad, 'cause it woulda set me straight. Like I said, things go wrong, you gotta improvise. Sure, you told Manny a story. But he ain't gonna buy it when I show up with the bag. 'Betso's a bum but here's the money, boss. You want I should help? Or you wanna handle him yourself?' Get the picture, Frankie? I'm in and you're out."

I looked over at Roxanne and Linda, both of them gaping slack-jawed over what they correctly perceived as their own death warrant. Scarlo had to kill us. And the worse part was that, with us out of the way, his plan would probably work, temporarily. Even if Adonis didn't believe him, which he wouldn't, Scarlo's fairy tale would be a convenient out. Later, I was sure, Adonis would deal with Scarlo, quietly, privately.

I stood there, bleeding, devoid of rational thought, while Scarlo gave Nick and Sid their marching orders: "Do what you have to do. But get the fucking money!"

They hustled me out—no time for good-bye kisses—down the submarine-lit corridor with its red flocked walls and red carpet, past the desk man who gave new meaning to the word aloof, into the lot, and inside a Caddy. This one a two door.

They put me in the middle. Sid held the wheel and Nick held the gun. About all I had to hold was my breath. And that was knocked out of me by a sharp, unexpected punch to my sternum. Nick was setting the agenda: forget the express checkout Scarlo promised.

I considered touring the boroughs for a while, running them ragged while I played for time and an opportunity to escape. But extending my life by several hours was not a plus if they were going to be spent in the company of these two. I told Sid to head for the restaurant.

It took half an hour to get there. The Petrones didn't have much to say and I was in no mood for idle chatter. A thousand different scenarios were running through my mind and each one had the same ending: me dead and them laughing. By the time we arrived, I had it down to one. It took a slightly different route but unfortunately it ended the same way.

My only hope was Lieutenant Grimm. He just might have some men posted. If he did, I'd create a racket loud enough to gain their attention. There'd be a shoot out, of course, and some casualties. The question wasn't how many. But who?

As I'd expected, the place was closed and dark. They drove down the block a few times. With each pass my heart sank and my fears deepened. Not one miserable car. Not one lousy pedestrian. Nothing but rain. Maybe Grimm didn't care about his promotion.

"Looks clear," Nick said.

Sid pulled over. "All right, let's do it."

They hauled me out and dragged me along, my head swiveling in every direction. Still no sign of life. Goddamn that Grimm!

I unlocked the door and in we went. Sid pulled a flashlight from somewhere, aimed it at the bar and said, "Inside."

"No," Nick said. "The kitchen."

I didn't like the sound of it. Nick was pissed and my pain threshold was about to be tested.

I said, "It's not in the kitchen. It's in here."

"Get it!"

With the Petrones breathing down my neck I went behind the bar, opened the sliding panel and fished for the bag. Zilch. Nada. Bupkis. Nobody home.

Talk about panic. I skinned my knuckles as my hands flew around in the empty space.

"What the fuck?"

"Yeah," Nick said. "What the fuck." He grabbed my collar. "All right, smart ass, get up."

"It was here," I said. "I swear, it was right here."

He pushed me toward the kitchen. "In a way I'm glad," he said."

"Yeah," said his brother, beaming. "Me, too."

I figured I had two ways to go: I could check out with dignity. Or I could beg. There was no one around to write a citation for bravery, so I fell to me knees and began to plead. "Don't do it— I'll get the money—It's a mistake—Give me a break." Pitiful.

The litany was endless and the Petrones ate it up. The only thing I didn't do was cry. I think I was too scared to cry. I don't know. But when Sid Petrone dragged a chair toward one of the ovens, my tear ducts were sorely tested.

Funny how your mind works in the face of death. Mine was conjuring up an old movie with Jimmy Cagney. A tough guy on death row, he's asked by Father Pat O'Brien to save the Dead End Kids by showing cowardice on his way to the chair. Cagney refuses, then does it anyway, kicking and screaming while they strap him in. I never knew if that was an act or if the guy was really scared. Until now.

Tearing an apron into strips, they tied my hands behind the chair, my feet to its legs. Nick pulled some matches from his pocket, turned to his brother and said, "Get some oil."

My eyes popped when Sid hurried over with a gallon of Berio. They popped wider when he poured a healthy serving over my lap. I looked down as the oil seeped through my pants, into my crotch. I was about to be sauteed.

What does one do at a time like this? Pleading was out so I hit them with the old stand-by: "You'll never get away with this," I said. "Kill me and you'll never get the money."

"We ain't gonna kill you."

"Yeah," Sid agreed, grinning. He rolled a menu in the shape of a torch. "We're gonna make you mad, Fontana. Burn you up a little. Ha-ha!"

Nick ripped out a match. He lit it and I damn near fainted.

I could only imagine how I looked. The blood in my face wasn't draining, it was swirling inside my head like a Vegamatic. Nick fired up the torch and my blood stopped swirling. Somewhere inside, a plug was pulled, gravity took over and everything liquid went south.

Nick held the torch like Lady Liberty, its flame lighting up the kitchen like the Fourth of July. He waved it in front of my face. Sparks fell into my lap and I cringed with anticipation. But oil isn't gas, it takes longer to burn.

"I'll get it!" I shouted. "Let me go and I'll get it."

Meanwhile, Sid was busy pouring oil over the butcherblock counters. He'd rolled a few more menus, gave one to Nick and lit another.

"Where is it?" Nick said.

"It's under the bar!" I cried.

"You tried that. It ain't there." He looked to Sid. "Okay, Sid, let's make some heat. We're not gettin' nothin' from this fuck."

Sid dropped his torch on the counter and blew the hell out of my notion of oil versus gas. I heard a whooshing sound. Flames shot toward the ceiling. I had to turn my face from the heat. But not Sid. The guy had asbestos skin. Instead of backing away he moved closer, clapped his hands and giggled. Nick, too, was having a hard time controlling his glee. Two lunatics, having the time of their life. What a prize these boys must have been to their parents.

The flames got hotter, the temperature rose. Then it rained.

I turned my face upward and offered a prayer of thanks for all the fire codes ever written. But the rain was more of a mist. My sprinklers did their best but this was an angry fire, the heat so intense that already my hair was beginning to singe.

I was well beyond fear. Panic, terror, you name it. I screamed a meaningless plea for help while I wriggled and strained against the ropes. The chair teetered and fell. Nick was quick to set it right and once again I faced the fire.

But even this wasn't enough for him. He went to the oven, lowered the door, and turned on the gas.

"The way I figure it, Frankie, you got about three minutes. Come on, Sid, let's go."

They took off, the two of them pounding heavily across the kitchen floor, beyond my line of vision. I craned my neck. "Hold it!" I barked. "I'll get it. I'll get it right now. But shut it off!"

I couldn't believe they'd leave me like this. Surely they'd stop, douse the fire and give me one more chance. They had to. They couldn't risk blowing the money.

They didn't stop and come back.

I struggled, but it didn't help. I couldn't break loose and after awhile I found myself staring wide-eyed at the gaping restaurant oven, black and empty, except for a copper jet hissing gas like some nameless snake in a small, dark cave.

The fire raged, got closer, hotter. How long did I have? Minutes? Seconds?

Dying was one thing, getting my face blown off was something else. I couldn't take it. So I pushed off with my feet and began rocking the chair. Front and back, front and back at ever increasing angles, until finally the chair upended.

I was on my back, seat facing the oven. How fitting. To go out the way I'd lived: ass backward.

19

I had an aunt who died after a long battle with leukemia. With each setback they'd rush her to the hospital, and we, the family, would rush after her. I remember once, sitting at her bedside, thinking, "Please, don't let her die with me here alone." Just then her eyes fluttered. She reached out for my hand, squeezed it gently, and said very softly, "Not yet, Francis." Somehow my aunt knew it wasn't time.

From that day on I've always held the belief that you get a feeling about dying. That you know it's going to happen just before it happens—something you know for sure. I have no idea what that feeling might be like, but whatever it is, I definitely didn't have it. I was lying there completely vulnerable, with my face to the fire and my ass to the oven. I had no reason to think this wasn't the end, yet somehow I knew. It just wasn't my time.

Of course my blind faith did nothing to allay my wide-eyed

fear. The fire was closing in, the sprinkler mist fell with no effect, and the snake in the oven kept hissing. Like St. Thomas, I was having my doubts.

"Hold it right there!" It was a harsh voice with an unmistakable trace of Bed-Stuy.

I turned my face to the voice but couldn't see anyone. "Grimm!" I shouted. "In here. Here!"

But Sid and Nick had their own ideas.

"Over there!" Sid barked.

"Get 'em!" Grimm said. "Watch it!"

Bullets flew. They clanged the huge steel pots like clappers of cathedral bells.

Two shots were from close by. Then a retort, and another. The sound of shattered glass, tables overturning, men shouting, running. My kitchen was going up in smoke and my dining room was getting shot to hell. And what was I doing?

In days to come there'd be stories told about this, thrill seekers from every borough wanting a first-hand report: Where'd you say you were, Frankie?

My fight and here I was, tied to a chair. The whole thing was humiliating.

Not that I really wanted any part of it. I just wanted to see who was winning.

I twisted and bounced. The chair turned slightly. A little more bouncing and what I had was an end seat in the lodge, the action barely visible from the corner of one eye. I cursed but it didn't help. I squinted and that didn't help.

"Grimm! Grimm, for Chrissake, get me outta here!"

By now the kitchen was filled with smoke and I was soaked to the skin. Even with a good seat, I couldn't see the show in the dining room. But I could hear it. And smell it, along with the smoke—cordite and gas. And the sickly smell of the hair on my arm cooking. If I didn't get help soon, I'd be telling this story to the angels.

Suddenly a barrage of gun fire peppered the walls. An automatic of some kind. It hit close then moved away, blowing to bits everything in its wake. Oven parts and crockery flew. I thought for sure it would set off the oven, but it didn't.

"Fontana!" Grimm called. "You in here?"

"On the floor," I said. "By the oven. They got the gas on."

"Stay put," he said. "I'm coming."

Stay put! You had to love Grimm's sense of humor.

"I smell gas." A different voice.

" 'S'okay, the fire's out. Fontana! Yell out!"

"What the hell you think I' been doing. Keep coming!"

"We got 'em, lieutenant."

"Got who? I can't see shit."

"The Petrones. We got 'em."

"Fontana, you all right?"

"I can't move." My eyes stung.

"Get the medics! We got a man down here. I'm comin', Fontana. Fuckin' smoke. All right, all right, I see ya."

The concern on Grimm's face was downright touching. It wasn't enough that he'd saved my life, he thought I was hurt and was rushing to my aid. What a guy!

"Take it easy," he said, kneeling in the water, ruining his suit for me.

"I'm all right."

"You sure?"

"Yeah, yeah, I'm fine. Kill the gas and get me out of here, will you?"

He got to his feet and looked down at me in total disdain. "I told you, asshole. If you can't take the heat, get the hell outta the kitchen!"

"Yeah," I said. "Very funny."

It took an hour or so to rid the place of smoke, firemen, and the boys from Emergency Medical Service. The cops were another matter. Arson, assault, attempted murder, there was a list of felonies a yard long here. Not to mention the perps caught in the act. Biggies at that.

Among the bluecoats the mood was high. They buzzed in and out of Fontana's slapping backs and giving more high fives than a bowling league on Tuesday night. Even Grimm was elated, ruined suit and all. Until I stonewalled him.

"Whadaya mean you won't press charges?"

There were seven of us jammed in my office: Grimm, three of his men, myself, and the Petrones, cuffed and snarling like two rabid dogs. "You don't have to press charges," Grimm said. "We got 'em in the act."

"Fine. But don't expect me to testify."

"Whataya talkin' about? You gotta testify."

"Why?" I said innocently.

Grimm blinked and shook his head. "Why? You sayin' why? Ain't you the same guy who was beggin' for help? 'Grimm,'" he aped, " 'Grimm, in here!' And you ask why. What the hell you trying to pull here, Fontana?"

What I was pulling was the best card I'd had all night. In fact, my only trump. A way to eliminate Johnny Scarlo and his whole bloody crew. Not for one night, or six months, or whatever time they'd pull for what they did tonight. They'd come after me eventually and that I couldn't accept. To live happily ever after, I needed a permanent solution. Grimm, no matter what he said, could never assure me of the one basic ingredient I so desperately needed—peace of mind.

Lieutenant Grimm railed on: "You listen to me, you fuckin' ski-ball." He sounded vicious, worse than Sid and Nick at their meanest. Only Scarlo's boys weren't surprised by this act. Nobody rats on the mob. It's deaf and dumb all the way for a stand-up guy.

"You asked for help and I gave it. You'd be in pieces now if it wasn't for me. Dead, *morto!* You copy? Now you're sayin' go home, forget the whole fuckin' thing. Well it ain't gonna happen. I'm takin' them in and you're going with me. You're gonna file that complaint or I'll put you back in that chair and let them finish the job. You hear what I'm saying?"

"Absolutely."

"Good."

"But it won't fly."

"Whadaya mean, 'It won't fly?'"

"They didn't do it."

If Grimm were white he'd have been red. He flared his nostrils and glared toward his men like he wanted to melt them down.

"Take that garbage outta here," he said, gesturing toward Sid and Nick. "I wanna talk to this eightball. Alone!"

I was doing a number on Grimm's head. He didn't deserve it but I had no choice. This one you couldn't win with a simple arrest. You had to eradicate the enemy. Grimm could never do that. I couldn't either. But there was someone I knew who could. And he was out there, waiting.

"All right," Grimm said, "we're alone. Now say again. In English this time."

"It wasn't them," I said again. "Those three guys I told you about. Julie, Monk, and Eddie. They were leaning on me, wanted a piece of the place. Hell, Sid and Nick, they tried to save me."

"Hey, guy, you think all niggers are chumps? I was bustin' heads while you were still in Ohio chuckin' corn." He aimed his chin at the door. "Punks like them, I eat 'em up and shit 'em out. They don't say boo or who done it. They take it. You know why? 'Cause I'm tougher. Trouble with you, Fontana, you're more scared of them than me. Maybe that's my fault. I let guys like you play around too long. You don't even know the friggin' rules. You think I'm your guardian angel? I'm not, pal. Next to me those guys are pansies."

"I know you're tough, lieutenant. But I can't lie in court. I mean that's perjury."

"I shoulda known," Grimm said. "I had you pegged for a gutless guinea. I was right. But you forget, we saw them bring you in. Right across the street from that old bagel shop. Got the whole scene on video, too. You say it was three other guys. Where'd they come from, huh?"

"I don't know. They were here, that's all."

"That's all? That's shit. Who tied you up? Who lit the fire, turned on the gas?"

"I told you. Julie, Monk, and Eddie."

"Knock it off!"

"That's my story. I'm sticking with it."

"So where'd they go? How'd they get out, huh? Tell me that."

I said, "Julie, Monk, and—"

"Give me them names again and I'll bust your face. Goddamn it!"

He spun around and began pacing the office, three steps and back. Then he stopped, rolled his shoulders, straightened his collar and took a deep breath. A new approach. I waited.

"Listen to me, Frank." (Frank. Hmm.) "I know it's Scarlo put the squeeze on you. That's why you called me in the first place. I mean, it's his kinda play. The Petrones, they're grunts, that's all—ditch diggers. But they're high enough. We get them, we get Scarlo. Your problem's solved. You can trust me on this one. Take it right to the bank."

Right to the river bank was more like it. I hesitated, pretended to think it over. It was all an act but time was flying. Scarlo had the girls and I was going nowhere.

"Okay," I said. "I'll do it. I'll come down tomorrow and make a statement. That good enough for you?"

"You don't sound convincing." He shook his head. "No way."

"Look, Grimm, I'm tired. I'm pissed off and I'm dirty. I wanna go home and get some sleep. I'll do what you want but get off my case. All right?"

"You wanna sleep, eh? So do I. I wanna sleep like a baby. Like I been laid by Diana Ross."

"You have my word," I said.

He moved in close. At 6'5" and two hundred plus pounds, getting close to Grimm was an eclipse. He shoved his face in front of mine and gave me one of those probing looks cops are famous for. That all-knowing, all-seeing look; a squint, a smirk, a barely perceptible nod. Lieutenant Grimm, hardnosed pseudo-psychic, was divining my integrity.

Having performed with due diligence, Grimm finally backed away. He took a moment to measure his words. "You wouldn't be pulling my pork, would you, Frank? I wouldn't care for that much. Not from you, anyway. So I'll ask you one more question: can you sell your pasta without wine?"

The inference was clear. If I finked out, he'd pull my liquor license. I knew he could do it and I'd have one helluva time explaining that one to James.

I assured him again he had nothing to worry about.

"Okay," he said. "I'll keep a man with you. We'll both sleep better, believe me."

More problems. With Grimm's man all over me, I'd never shake free. "No way," I said. "You bailed me out and I'm grateful, I really am. But you can't watch me for the next ten years. I can't live in a vacuum. I won't."

He nodded. "Don't tell me you're growing up? Well, you gotta start somewhere, I guess." He stuck out his hand. I pumped it. "All right, Frank Fontana. You're on your own." He turned to leave.

I knew damn well Grimm was lying. He'd never cut me loose with Scarlo out there. Grimm wasn't my guardian angel but he knew me well enough. With my track record I wasn't safe at a scout jamboree. I needed protection from myself, for Christ's sake. Besides, it wasn't just Scarlo that Grimm wanted to catch. It was the big fish himself, the collar to beat all previous collars, the quintessential bust. Manny Adonis.

I couldn't operate with a tail I couldn't shake and I couldn't shake a tail I couldn't see, so I caught Grimm as he was going.

"Yo, Grimm." He stopped. "Listen," I said, shuffling my feet, contrite in recanting my exclamation of new-found bravery. "I'll take that man if the offer's still good."

He grinned broadly, gleaming enamel and a single gold cap. "I had you covered," he said. Then he laughed and slapped my back. "Don't sweat it, kid, you'll get there." He turned his big head. "Thompson!" he called.

Thompson, one of the cops who was in my office, waved his hand.

"Yeah," Grimm said, "come 'ere a minute."

Thompson bounded over.

"Like you to meet Frank Fontana. Don't worry, he's found the right side. Stay with him till morning. See he gets down in one piece. He shits, you hand him paper. You got that?"

"Check," said Thompson.

"Okay, Frank, we're all set. See you tomorrow."

Grimm left after a handshake and a big smile. He took his crew with him. All but Thompson, a sandy haired, apple cheeked kid who looked more like a bellhop than a cop. If I couldn't shake Thompson I'd go back to accounting — if I ever got the chance.

I told Thompson to grab a coke at the bar, that I wanted time to assess the damage. He gave me a dubious look but went nonetheless. "I'll be right here if you need me."

"Check," I said.

Part of the ruse was to free up for a phone call. But I guess my instincts had become entrepreneurial because I did, in fact, check the damage, which wasn't too bad once the smoke cleared. The main counter was shot, some inventory lost, and a new paint job was badly needed. So was an insurance claim, to which I would add the cost of a new bathroom. The bullet holes I'd keep for a conversation piece. A bit of character for what was already an unsavory joint.

I phoned Sally.

" 'lo," came a groggy voice.

"Good morning."

"Oh, no."

"I'm beginning to think you don't love me anymore, Sal."

"What time is it?"

"Four a.m."

"I wouldn't care if you were Burt Reynolds," she said. "At four a.m. I hate the world. What is it this time, Frankie?"

"How'd you like a vacation?" I said.

"Paid?"

"Of course."

"I'd love it."

"You got it."

"That why you called? Jeez, you *are* crazy."

"Thanks," I said. "But that's not why I called."

"I knew it."

"Look, shake the sand from your eyes and get down here right away."

"The joint?"

"Yeah, We had a small fire."

"*Fire?* For Chrissake, Frankie. What—"

"Later. I need your car so get down here, all right? And listen, there's a cop here I'm trying to shake. Park your car in the back and come in the front. Keep him busy while I slip out."

"Ah, Jesus."

"Yeah, I know. They never covered this in bartender's school. Now get with it. I'll watch from the kitchen window."

I hung up and started out for the kitchen. There were voices coming from the bar area. I stopped to listen. Thompson was telling someone that she couldn't come in. Who the hell was that at four in the morning? I went up front to check it out.

"Joanne!" I hollered.

Thompson spun around. "She says she works here."

"Yeah," I said. "Let her pass."

"Like, wow!" Joanne declared. "I don't believe this."

She was wearing high heels and a thigh-length party dress. I said, "What the hell are *you* doing here?"

"I was on my way home from a date," she said, patting both sides of her new hairdo. "I always pass this way, through the midtown tunnel and out on Borden Avenue. I saw the fire trucks." She shook her head. "Man, what a mess!"

"Tell me about it."

"Sally's gonna have a fit."

"Yeah," I said. I was the owner and she was worried about Sally.

She said, "It took almost a whole day to clean up that other mess. Went home exhausted, all of us."

"Wait a minute," I said. "You helped?"

"Why? Is that time and a half?"

"Come here," I said. "I wanna show you something. Pardon us a minute, will you, Thompson?"

He shrugged.

I took Joanne behind the bar. She had to tiptoe through the wreckage. "I'm gonna ruin my shoes," she moaned.

"Look here," I said, stooping down, gesturing toward the empty compartment under the bar. "There was a bag in here the other day."

"Gym bag," she said without hesitation. "All bashed up, soaked with booze, with some dirty socks balled up in it?"

I howled.

"Frankie! Frankie, what's the matter?"

My heart did flips. "Whadya do with the bag?" I said excitedly.

"I did what Sally wanted," she said. "I threw it out with all the other debris."

20

I hurried out to the back on the chance the bag was in the dumpster. I didn't remember the pick-up days but it didn't matter. I'd been using a carting company owned by the mob and their collection days were as unpredictable as their management. The guys on the truck spent more time collecting money at the track than garbage at restaurants.

My hopes were high as I checked the dumpster. It was empty. The money was landfill by now. The bottom of my stomach was trying to turn over.

My out money. Three hundred and fifty grand, tossed in the garbage. What the hell was I going to tell Adonis and Betso: Sorry, guys, the bread's been eighty-sixed by an anal compulsive clean freak?

Meanwhile, Detective Thompson was guzzling his third coke, getting juiced on caffeine, and antsy in the process. I was antsy too. My scheme was falling apart and I still had two women to rescue from the jaws of death.

By the time I spotted Sally's car from the kitchen window, it was still night, but just barely. I wanted desperately to grill her about the money, but Detective Thompson was hawking me from the bar and all I could do was stand by helplessly while Sally trotted up the block and around the corner.

Thompson heard her at the door and rushed for the intercept. While they exchanged pleasantries, I beat it out the back.

Sally's car was in worse shape than my Skyhawk. An old Duster she'd wrested from her ex-husband. It wasn't much to show for a five-year marriage but then it was a helluva lot more than I'd gotten from mine. The keys were in the ignition. And it started right up.

Once again I searched the streets for a phone. Being roused at dawn wouldn't make Adonis any happier than Sally Plunk. But guys like him don't know from nine to five, they work all hours. Hell, their best work is done between three and five a.m.

I found a phone on the way to Brooklyn. The same guy answered. "Seven, eight, five." Nothing groggy in *his* voice. He sounded sharper than before. He'd better be.

This time I ignored protocol. If the phone was tapped, fuck it. "This is Frank Fontana," I said. "The guy who called before. You blew it, pal. You gave the message to Scarlo instead of Manny. Now we're both in the shitter. So get Adonis out of bed and tell him I'm waiting for him in front of his club. And don't worry, he'll love you for it."

He started to squawk. I hung up. Negatives I didn't need. I had to think positive, and believing Adonis would show was the first step.

Maybe these guys sleep in their clothes. At 4:55, eighteen minutes after I'd called, Adonis pulled up.

He seemed anxious, he and his people. They'd brought two sets of wheels and the apes hit the sidewalk while the cars were still in motion, their doors slamming, one after the other, bang-bang-bang like gunshots.

Once, years ago, I'd killed an off day at one of those drive-through zoos in Jersey. The kind that warns you to keep your windows closed and don't feed the animals — as if anyone was wacky enough to try. I had to stop at one point while a band of furry things with drooling mouths surrounded my car and made jungle noises at me. It's the way I felt that morning in front of the Greenpoint Social Club.

Within seconds Manny's boys had my car encircled and me pegged for a light breakfast. I waved my fingers at them. They snarled.

I was about to lock my doors when Manny Adonis showed. It was the first time I'd ever seen him in casual wear, slacks and open shirt. It did nothing to soften his demeanor. I didn't wait for his invitation.

"This better be good," he said, as I got out of the car and was abruptly lifted off my feet.

"It's better than good," I said, wiggling my toes in search of terra firma.

"Put him down," Manny said.

He waved his boys away and motioned for me to get closer. He wanted a private talk. Me and the boss chatting at five a.m. on a quiet sidewalk in Brooklyn. Had I arrived, or what? So why was I shaking?

"I heard what happened," he said. "About the call last night. Johnny hangs there once in awhile. I should have remembered that. So what happened?"

I gave him the run down, from the meet with Julie to the fire at dawn. He found the story amusing. In particular, the way the girls and I had handled the Petrones. I thought he'd be pissed over Lieutenant Grimm's involvement, but he wasn't. In fact, he seemed pleased.

"He's got the girls, eh?" he said.

"Yeah," I said. "Him and two other guys."

"This other one. You say she's her sister?"

"From Denver," I said. "But she's only in this to help her sister. You'll let her go, won't you?"

"Depends," Manny said. "On her sister. She gonna sing pretty songs?"

I wanted to protect Linda but her safety was out of my hands and squarely in Roxanne's. "She'll sing," I said. "Lullabyes."

Adonis smiled. "She'd better," he said. "All right, we're going. You'll ride with me."

I smiled back at him. "Thanks, but I've got a car."

His smile dropped away. "It's too early for jokes, Fontana."

It wasn't the first time in my life I'd been taken for the proverbial ride. But this time my heart wasn't in my throat. It wasn't me they were going to waste. I felt safe and secure. Almost smug. Scarlo was about to catch his lumps and I'd be there to see it. That's when it hit me.

Whoever said knowledge is power didn't know beans about wiseguys. If anything's the kiss of death it's knowing too much. I knew enough right now to increase my insurance premiums and I hadn't even witnessed the grand finale. My heart started to rise.

It also began to dawn on me that we weren't headed for Sheepshead Bay and the Briny. I turned to Adonis. He was seated next to me, eyes closed, head back like he didn't have a worry in the world.

"Excuse me," I said.

He kept his eyes shut and rolled his head casually. "Hmm?"
I said, "I may be wrong, but aren't we going the wrong way?
The Briny's in the other direction."

"I know," he said.

I could barely swallow. My palms were cold and clamy and I
envisioned myself being taken away, hand in hand with the one
man I hated most in the world. This wasn't what I'd had in mind.

I coughed and said, "Could I ask where we're going?"

He opened his eyes. They were red and watery. "Johnny moved
the show to Howard Beach," he said. "A shack on the channel."

"How do you know that?"

He rubbed the tip of his nose. "You don't think I'd let him run
loose, do you? I knew where he was before *you* did."

"He took the girls?"

Manny nodded. "Don't worry. They're still on their feet."

Don't worry. Easy for him to say. "Gees," I said.

"What are you nervous about? Isn't this what you wanted?"

"Sure, but . . . well, you know . . ."

Adonis patted my knee. "You'll be all right. Just tell me in
front of Scarlo what you told me alone. His girlfriend'll do the
rest. You don't know it, Fontana, but you're helping me here,
making a friend. Maybe two if you count Betso."

I gulped.

"I talked to him last night," Manny said. "Told him I had a line
on his dough. I had to eat some crow but it was worse for him. You
should have heard him when I asked how he'd let himself be taken
by a guy like you." He shook his head. "That friggin' Johnny. I got
a year's worth of time invested in Betso's operation and that clown
almost blows it over a few lousy bucks."

"A few lousy bucks?" I said.

He shrugged. "Everything's relative. Funny thing about it, I
would have bailed him out if he'd come to me. But no. Let me tell

you something, Frankie, about this new breed. It's not enough they got it all. They want more. How do you get more when you've got everything? If it isn't drugs, it's gambling, gay bars, kiddie porn. Not like the old days. Vito would have broken all their bones for what passes for normal operations today."

He paused and gazed out the window. "Stupid," he said. "Real stupid."

I wondered what he'd say if he knew Betso's money was on its way to a dump in Staten Island. Maybe it *was* only a few lousy bucks, but when I closed my eyes I could hear him saying, "Stupid. Real stupid."

It didn't take us long to reach Howard Beach. A tight little neighborhood, it was mostly private homes for blue collar workers, family men who longed for beach front property but had to settle for homes on brackish canals, clogged arteries of what used to be the moving tides of Pumpkin Patch Channel and Grassy Bay. Colorful names for the way it was before the dredgers came in and mucked it all up.

I was trying to picture Scarlo's hide out, when Adonis said, "There it is."

We parked and I peered out.

"Okay, Fontana," Manny said. "You're on."

We got out. I took a deep breath. The air was damp and smelled of dead fish. A gravel driveway sloped downward to the water's edge. About halfway down, an old inboard was perched on a trailer. Alongside the boat, a wooden staircase led to a badly listing deck—and Scarlo's shack.

Adonis nudged me. "You go first," he said.

I started to walk. My legs felt like they were connected with rubber bands. I swayed and teetered my way across the gravel as if the ground was the deck of a rolling ship. I wanted Scarlo to go down but I didn't want to see it happen.

Manny's boys were behind me. "What do I do?" I whispered over my shoulder.

No response.

Great. On-the-job-training. I wanted no part of it. One look at Adonis and Johnny Scarlo was bound to flip. All I could picture were guns and blood. Their guns, my blood.

The walk down that driveway took forever. I felt like part of the Earp family on the way to the O.K. Corral. And there I was, unarmed.

With me leading the way, we went single file up the staircase. It creaked and moaned under our feet. I didn't see any windows, but I did see a door. We stopped and fanned out. They flanked the door, six, including Manny. Mr. Adonis exercised the privilege of rank by taking a position at the rear. I stood in the middle, staring glassy-eyed at the door.

Manny leaned out, cupped his ear and motioned for me to listen. I pressed my ear to the door. Nothing.

"Knock," he whispered.

I knocked.

Footsteps. Then Scarlo. "Who is it?"

"Frankie," I said. There was something wrong with my volume control. My mouth had moved but little came out. I cleared my throat and tried again. *"Frankie!"* I said in a booming voice that carried across the channel.

Scarlo undid the latch—or cocked a piece—and opened the door. He had a gun in his hand. His eyes shifted from side to side. I could see the questions in his shady countenance: How'd you find me? What happened to Sid and Nick?

But none of this was said. Instead, someone shoved me from behind. So hard that my arms flew out and I left my feet like a free-falling parachutist on his maiden flight. For a short flight, it had one helluva landing.

Scarlo never fired. Maybe there wasn't time. But the gun came up as we collided. Then I did what I do best: hit the floor.

Manny's boys were stepping all over me. They had Scarlo turned around and the gun he was holding had fallen next to my face. I reached for it and felt two hundred pounds of shoe on my hand. Then the gun disappeared.

"In the chair," Adonis was saying, all calm and unfazed.

For a moment I thought he meant me, that he wanted to help me. But they weren't helping anyone. I heard a grunt from Scarlo, followed by a heavy thud.

Then one of Scarlo's boys spoke up: "What's goin' on?"

"That's up to you," Adonis said nonchalantly.

"Whadaya mean? He says, 'Come,' we come. Ain't you callin' this?"

"Whadaya you think?"

"Jeez, I mean, we thought—you know—like you're the boss, and, well,—he says, 'Work,' we figure it's you callin' the shot."

"Then bury the hardware."

"Sure. Sure thing, Mr. Adonis."

With great effort I hauled myself to my feet. The fight was over. They had Scarlo in a chair against the wall, under a trophy. It was some kind of shark. A maneater.

I looked at Scarlo. He was sitting there, casually running a toothpick under his fingernails. I have to admit I admired his style.

Roxanne, however, was a different case. She was backed in the corner, her eyes red and swollen, clutching her sister who'd moved in beside her. Even with Linda's support, I could see she was terrified.

"All right," Adonis said.

Game time, I thought.

"Fontana's gonna tell us a story. We're all gonna listen and no one opens their mouth until it's over." This last comment he directed at Scarlo who was eyeing me up like the shark mounted on the wall.

Manny Adonis looked at me. "Skip the 'Once upon a time,'" he said. "Start with the bet."

I told the story with flourish, incriminating Scarlo wherever I could, while at the same time softening the involvement of his unknowing accomplice, Roxanne Ducharme. She'd been taken in, as I had been taken, all of it part of a scheme to get the bookies off Scarlo's back. I closed the tale with a strong but sentimental plea for Roxanne's absolution. By the time I'd finished, the Dorsey girls were trading handkerchiefs.

I stepped back. The rest was up to Roxanne.

Manny called her over but the girl didn't move. Scarlo had her fixed with a penetrating glare, a telepathic message between lovers that neither Manny or I could ever compete with.

She cocked her head for a moment as if contemplating her decision. That he'd threatened to kill her didn't seem to matter. She really loved this maniac, and for one hair-raising moment I thought she'd go along with him. I think if Linda hadn't been there, she would have.

But Linda kept at her, guiding her gently but firmly out of that corner of her life in which she'd buried herself.

Encouraged by her sister, Roxanne announced in a clear voice: "Everything Frankie said is true."

Scarlo erupted.

He sprang to his feet, ranted and raved, threw his arms in the air and kicked the chair. But Scarlo wasn't pleading for his life. He was too incensed to plead for anything except perhaps five minutes alone with Roxanne and me. Roxanne was a back stabbing whore and I was a dumb bastard with more luck than I deserved. How he figured that I'd never know.

Scarlo was nailed. What I had to do was get out of there before Adonis remembered the money. So far, nothing serious had happened, no one had been hurt. But it wouldn't be long. I could see it in Adonis's face, the dreamy look of a killer weighing his options. It wouldn't be enough to shoot Scarlo dead. He deserved something much more creative, a new chapter in the *Hitman's Handbook*, something the boys at the club would kick around for years to come.

I cleared my throat and Adonis snapped out of his reverie. He smiled and nodded several times as if totally satisfied with his decision. Manny was happy. At least for now. Which definitely wasn't the case with Scarlo. His breathing was strained and he'd developed the pallor of a dying fish.

It was time to check out, to leave the boys to their fun. As for me, my only hope was to hit the state Lotto between now and tomorrow morning.

21

"Thank God that's over," Linda said.

"I believe in God as much as the next guy," I said. "But if He wants my thanks He'll have to do better than this."

It was the first piece of conversation we'd had since one of Manny's boys had dropped us off. Adonis had been gracious enough to offer a lift to our car. Why not? With seven men on his team, he could afford to give up a few.

We were in the front seat of Sally's car, Linda on the flank, Roxanne in the middle, wasting good tears and babbling about what might have been. It wasn't worth telling her that it wasn't worth it, so we let her cry herself out.

My response about God had apparently given Linda something to think about. She leaned forward and said, "It *is* over, isn't it?"

"Yeah," I said sullenly. "It's over."

Of course it wasn't over. It wouldn't be until the small matter of
Betso's money was resolved. Adonis had summed it up perfectly.
As we were leaving, he'd pulled me aside. "Aren't you forgetting
something? Three hundred large?" He'd grinned at me. "I'll be
around to see you. Who knows? You may get outta this yet."

I would have gone directly to Fontana's. But the girls were
bushed and I wanted to set them up in the loft before going back.
There was little chance I'd find the money but looking for it would
give me a feeling of purpose, something to do when there was
nothing left to do except wait. If the place wasn't wrecked by now,
it would be after I turned it upside down. Maybe I could back
track to the garbage dump.

"I wanna go home," Roxanne said.

"Not as much as I do," I said. "But you heard the man. He
wants you and me to be available. You may not like it, Rox, but
we're still partners."

She looked at me with red-rimmed eyes. "Would it do any good
to say I'm sorry?"

"Sure, if you want. You were hurt as much as I was. Maybe
more. It's too bad our lives are controlled by hormones."

"Amen," Linda said.

Roxanne sniffled. "Why can't I ever fall for a man like you?"
she said. Then she kissed my cheek and placed her head on my
shoulder. Linda smiled and patted her hand. I thought about how
I could raise three hundred, fifty thousand dollars, quick.

We rode the elevator in silence, each of us too whipped to say
anything. I didn't have to see myself in a mirror to know I looked
like shit. My clothes were shot and could not have smelled worse
if I'd taken a swim in the East River. I figured by this time Scarlo
would be doing just that.

I expected to find the loft hot and musty. I also expected to find the door and windows locked. The windows were open and so was the door.

I was about to ask Linda if she'd left it this way when a familiar voice resonated from the bedroom: "I sure hope that's you, Fontana."

The girls went pale and froze in the doorway. I shook my head, meaning, Don't worry. Fontana the optimist.

"What are *you* doing here?" I asked Lieutenant Grimm as he shambled into view, his huge frame blocking the breeze from the windows.

"You want a hint? Or would you rather guess it cold?"

He eyed the girls and nonchalantly shook his oversized skull. "Never enough hours in the day, huh, Frankie? They the reason you ducked out on Thompson? That kid'll be working the South Bronx playgrounds because of you."

"I'm sorry to hear that," I said. "He's a nice kid."

"You're so fulla shit," Grimm said. He walked over to me, looked me up and down and wrinkled his nose. "You even smell like it. I don't know about you. I mean I've met chronic liars before. But you're the chronic lie. Everything you say is bullshit. Your whole life is bullshit. Now suppose you tell me where you ran off to. Not that I'll believe it."

"I had a date."

He nodded toward the girls. "With them?"

"Come on, Grimm. You knew I'd never kiss and tell."

"You will when you kiss my ass. I've had it with you, Fontana. I got two ex-wives and two lawyers on my back. I got a daughter who hates me and a son who hates college. That's grief in spades, and if you wise crack, I'll belt you. But I'll tell you something, all of that, it's nothing compared to you."

"I'm sorry you feel that way, Lieutenant. But I couldn't stand them up. Could I, ladies?"

"No," said Roxanne, straight-faced.

Linda went frisbee-eyed. "Lieutenant?"

"Excuse me," I said. "Linda, Roxanne, I'd like you to meet a true champion of justice. Lieutenant Grimm, N.Y.P.D."

"I'd like to sit down," Linda said.

"Don't be fooled by his name." I smiled. "He's really a sweet guy."

"Yeah," Grimm snickered. "I'm an all-day sucker. I spend the morning knockin' heads with Sid and Nick Petrone while you're knockin' around with two beautiful women. And look at you, for Chrissake!" He rolled his eyes. "Where the hell did *I* go wrong? All right, enough'a this crap. Let's sit down and sort this out."

We sat at the kitchen counter sorting it out. Roxanne, who was more accustomed to lies, spoke for herself and her sister. We'd spent the past few hours in a motel in Brooklyn. She didn't know the name. But it was great and so was I. Like I always say, if you have to lie, make it a beauty.

Grimm didn't like the story half as much as I did. Especially the hot parts. Not too graphic but spicy enough to titillate. By the time it was over, Grimm was sorry he'd asked.

With Linda feeding him coffee, Grimm waited while I took a shower. I was going downtown to give him the statement he wanted. It was the least I could do for the guy. He didn't know it but the big fish had slipped the hook. No way he'd catch Adonis. And Scarlo, who was second best, was already stuffed and mounted by now. About all that was left for Lieutenant Grimm were the Petrones. And he wouldn't have them very long. Adonis would see to that. He'd have them out on bail in one hour. They'd be dead in two. It was a jungle out there.

It looked as though Grimm would have nothing to show for his trouble except a bruised ego. It wasn't the way you repay a guy who had saved your life. I'd never admit it to Grimm, but he was right about one thing: I was definitely more afraid of his competitors than I could ever be of him.

Downtown I had to sign my name in a dozen places and swear a dozen times to everything Grimm wanted me to swear to. I was the victim of an extortion scheme masterminded by one John Scarlo. His top aides, the brothers Petrone, whom I'd seen many times with Scarlo, had torched my place to convince me. I gave dates, times and dialogue. Cooperation was the key word and I gave it willingly. By the time it was over, there was more horseshit in Grimm's office than in the stables of the mounted police.

"You better stay here till we pick him up," Grimm told me.

I wanted to tell him he'd best notify the Department of Social Security. If finding Scarlo was the sole criterion for going home, I'd be sitting in his office until my sixty-fifth birthday.

"How about this?" I countered. "Get Thompson back from the Bronx. Let him stay with me. What the hell, he deserves another chance."

Eventually Grimm agreed. "But stay close to him this time. You wanna get laid, let him watch. I won't lie to you, Frankie. You're in a tough spot long as Scarlo's alive." He gave me an encouraging pat. "Can you handle it?"

I was about to respond when one of Grimm's men barged in. He seemed excited. Grimm seemed annoyed. "Can't you see I'm busy?"

"You're gonna want this, Lieutenant."

"For Chrissake, Hodge. All right, what is it?"

"Joe Tate on line one," Hodge said. "Says he got a snitch with a hot tip about Betso."

Grimm shot me a look. I shrugged.

He picked up the phone. "Lieutenant Grimm."

Grimm listened awhile. He nodded his head a few times. Then his eyes got wide. "Hold it! Lemme write that down." He pulled a sheet of paper in front of him, held it in place with his elbow, and began writing furiously. "J & L's Body/Fender," he said. "Hoboken. Two o'clock sharp. Got it!"

I'd inched forward in my seat, curious but not alarmed. "What's going on?" I asked.

"Stay put," Grimm said. He got up. "Hodge, come with me."

They went outside Grimm's office and closed the door behind them. I could see them beyond the glass partition. Grimm's hands were flying all over the place, giving orders to Detective Hodge who was taking notes, bouncing his head up and down while he scribbled.

A few moments later Grimm was back. He positioned himself directly in front me. I had to strain my neck to see his face. I looked up and what I saw was the inside of his nostrils. They were flared.

"It's goin' down," he said.

They packed me in the back seat of an unmarked car and we headed for Hoboken. Whatever it was that we were getting into, it had setup written all over it. I knew it and so did Grimm. But Grimm wasn't talking. Not to me, anyway. He was too busy giving orders on the radio. I listened, duly impressed.

Grimm wasn't taking any chances. In addition to his own crew, he arranged for a S.W.A.T team and a back up by the Hoboken P.D. He even ordered a helicopter.

As for my role, I wasn't sure until Grimm turned to me and said, "I can't wait to see Betso's face when I drag *you* out."

22

I & L's Body/Fender was a long, flat-roofed garage on a dead end street flanked by abandoned warehouses and loading bays. There were no trucks and no people around. Just the Hoboken police, who were waiting for us at the corner.

Hodge pulled over and Grimm got out. I could hear radios crackling. I looked around for the S.W.A.T. boys. I couldn't see them but I knew they were here. On the roofs, maybe, laying low, guns ready.

Grimm looked at his watch and waved us out. We gathered around him: Hodge and I, plus a half dozen cops. They seemed eager.

Grimm said, "It's five minutes to two. We'll go on foot. Hodge, stay here with Fontana. I'll call you when I want him." He winked at Hodge. "Keep him safe."

"All right," Grimm said, "Let's get it done."

I inched closer to Hodge and watched them move down the block. There were five cops, including Grimm. He had the lead, hunched over like he had a problem with his back. They stayed close to the buildings. About fifty yards away was J & L. In the front, was a set of broad doors that pulled up from the bottom. One of them had a smaller door inset in the middle. It was open.

Grimm wasted no time. He put his radio to his mouth and said something. I looked up and saw a row of heads appear on the roofs across the street. He checked them out, gripped his gun in both hands, and ran in. His men followed.

I waited for gunshots.

Nothing. Silence, except for Hodge who muttered, "It's a wash out. Goddamn it!"

"Yeah," I said.

I'd hardly had time to relax when one of Grimm's men reappeared. He'd poked his head out the door and was waving at us.

Hodge said, "That's us, Fontana. Come on, move it!"

Hodge hussled down the block. I tried to keep pace but my heart wasn't in it.

It was a big garage loaded with cars, mostly imports. They were new and shiny, and undoubtedly hot.

I didn't see anyone at first. Then Grimm shouted, "Over here, Hodge!"

Weaving our way among the cars, Hodge steered me toward the sound of Grimm's voice. We found him in the back, alongside a pair of hydraulic lifts. One of the lifts was elevated, a Porsche turbo sitting on top. Below the Porsche was a grease pit.

Grimm stood at the edge of it, staring down with keen interest. I didn't see his men but I could hear them. They were down in the pit.

". . . not much of his face left, Lieutenant. But it's Scarlo, that's for sure."

"What about Fatso?" Grimm said. "Can he talk?"

"Yes, Sir," came the voice. "But he ain't gonna."

"We'll see," Grimm said. "Get him up here!"

Meanwhile, I'd sidled up to Grimm. He threw me a glance and said, "Take a look, Frankie."

When I was a kid, years ago, my brother James took me to a carnival. It had a freak show that featured the Headless Man. I looked down. What I saw bore a striking resemblance.

Scarlo was stretched out in a pool of grease. I could tell he was on his back by the way his feet were pointing. There was too much blood to see anything else.

"Jesus," I said. My face flushed.

They were coming up out of the pit, Grimm's men and Fat Alfie Betso. They'd cuffed his hands behind his back. He seemed disoriented, stumbling once as he made his way up the steps. When he reached the top I saw blood trickle down the side of his face.

Grimm shook his head. "Sloppy," he said to Betso. "Very sloppy."

Betso growled. It came from way down, deep in his chest, like a hungry bear.

"Whats'a matter?" Grimm said. "Not awake yet?" He turned to one of his men. "Show him the gun, Niland. Let's see if that wakes him up."

Keeping his distance, Niland produced a white handkerchief, within which was a rather large revolver.

Grimm said, "We took it from *your* hand, Betso. Whadaya think? We got a case or don't we?"

Betso stared at the gun. "They set me up," he said.

"Who's they?" Grimm said.

"Fuck you!" Betso said.

Hodge was off to one side, Niland the other. Grimm was about six feet away from Betso. I was six yards behind Grimm, and inching backward.

"Fontana!" Grimm called over his shoulder.

Betso roared, lowered his head and charged.

Grimm went down. Hodge and Niland closed in. They hit Betso and bounced off. It was up to me now. Three hundred pounds of runaway blubber was coming right at me.

I got up on my toes and gave him a head fake. Left, then right. He bellowed and took the first fake. I jumped to one side, threw myself on the ground and stuck out my foot. It caught his ankle. Down he went. Simple.

I guess it doesn't take much to win cops over. Hodge liked my moves. So did Niland. "He showed a lot'a guts," he said to Grimm.

Grimm knew better but he allowed me to wallow in flattery. In fact, he offered a stroke of his own. "Nice work, hump head."

You had to like the guy.

I liked him even more after he had Betso taken away. "It was a bad idea," he said, "bringing you here. You could'a got hurt."

"Didn't know you cared, Lieutenant."

He shook his head. "I don't know how you pulled it off, Fontana. But I'll trade Scarlo for Betso any day of the week."

"Believe me," I said, "I had nothing to do with it."

"You never do. Yet somehow you're always in the middle of things. What's amazing is the way you wriggle out of it. Were you always like that?"

I smiled at him. "I couldn't do it without your help."

"Yeah," Grimm said. "First the Petrones, now these two."

"What happened with Sid and Nick?" I said.

He shrugged. "My guess? They're doin' a Jacques Cousteau in

203

Jamaica Bay. So you see, Fontana, your problems are over. I got my bust and you got your place back. Everyone's happy. Hey, you ever need me again, just give a holler."

"Yours'll be the first call."

He took my arm and the two of us walked slowly out of J & L Body/Fender.

"Oh," Grimm said, "by the way."

By the way. I hate those by-the-ways.

"The D.A.'ll want you to come in. We got a good case against Betso. But I know the D.A. He'll wanna firm it up. He'll want a motive. I'm gonna tell him, 'Anybody can do it, you can.' You'll talk to him, won't you, Frank?"

23

Fontana's Restaurant resembled some union hall during a contract dispute. Arguments, shouting, phones ringing off the wall. The chefs refused to work under these conditions. The dining room was still a mess and the waitresses weren't about to set it right. The kitchen help thought the fire was set by the Immigration Department in a plot to pull their green cards. The busboys were at the bar getting sloshed.

What my staff needed was leadership. I looked around for Sally Plunk.

Joanne spotted me and came running over. She was waving an early edition of the New York *Post*. The fire had made page three on the strength of the shootout.

"Did you see this?" she said, bubbling with excitement.

"I don't have to see it," I said. "I was here. Remember? Somebody get the phone."

"We did for a while," Joanne said. "But like, what's the sense?"

I went to the phone and picked it up. "Fontana's."

"Oh, *good!* You're open." A woman's voice. She sounded thrilled. "I'd like a table for twenty. About eightish? Near the bullet holes, if that's possible."

Table for twenty. Too bad I wasn't shot. We'd be standing room only for a year. "Call again next week," I said and hung up.

"It's been like that all morning," said Joanne. "We didn't know what to say so we stopped answering."

"Where's Sally?"

"Fort Lauderdale."

"What?"

"Sure. You told her to take a vacation. How about me?"

"Wait a minute, back up. Sally went to Lauderdale?"

"This morning. She called me at home. It's okay, isn't it? I mean you told her to go. So what do you say? Can I go, too? Jeez, a paid vacation. I haven't had one'a those in years."

"Forget it," I said. "We're going to straighten the place out. I want the bar open as soon as possible. Until the kitchen's ready we'll feed 'em pretzels and nuts. Now, about Sally. Did she leave a number?"

"She said she'd call *you.*"

"When?"

"When she gets back. Oh, about her car. She'd like you to have the oil changed."

It took thirteen hours to clean up. The kitchen required major surgery and wouldn't fully recover for several weeks. But the bar looked presentable and on the second night we opened for business.

Everyone had helped to get the place ready. Except the chefs. Those temperamental bastards claimed their hands were too valuable to risk on manual labor. Even Linda pitched in. Roxanne would have helped, too. But she was too busy rearranging her life. Apparently the torch she carried for Scarlo bore a low flame.

During the clean up I wouldn't allow anyone to throw anything out before showing it to me. I knew the bag had been tossed but I just had to check anyway. They thought I was crazy, shell shocked from what was now a legendary gunfight. I told them everything in the place had sentimental value.

Nothing turned up. Not a shred.

What did surface were the pain-in-the-ass suburbanites in their B.M.W.'s. The upwardly mobile middle-class thrill seekers, chasing headlines in their Gucci's and neo-classic Claibornes. I don't know what the hell they expected to find. They were the kind of clientele my brother would have approved of. Not a concealed weapon or crooked nose among them.

For five consecutive nights we catered to civilians and Fontana's made its run to fame and fortune. On the sixth night we died. Why? Who knows.

I just knew that while the gentry were around, Adonis wouldn't be. I had no idea what he was planning to do about the money or Betso, but it wouldn't be long before he showed his face.

It was ten o'clock on the sixth night. The place was a morgue. I was polishing glasses, chatting with Linda. Roxanne was in my office, napping. The door opened and Bobby Chubbs waddled in.

He offered a feeble wave and took a stool at the opposite end. "Gimme a double anything," he said as I approached.

"Beefeaters?"

He gave a disconsolate nod. "Write offs," he said. "One thing I hate is write offs."

I knew what he meant. Scarlo's untimely demise had cost Chubbs a small fortune. I gave him his drink.

He sighed. "I hated that sonofabitch when he was alive. Now he's dead, I hate him worse. I should'a known."

"You and me both," I said.

Chubbs rolled his eyes. "You don't know shit, Frank." He glanced over at Linda, motioned me closer. "C'mere." I leaned in. "I'll tell ya, kid. I wasn't gonna take his action. I was cuttin' him off, ya know? Then I get this call. 'Give him what he wants or you're outta business.' Fuckin' Adonis, man. Like he's gonna back up the guy. I should'a known."

"Wait a minute," I said. "Adonis knew? Why didn't you tell me before?"

"What for?" Chubbs squealed. "What difference? I'm piped and so are you."

Well put, I thought. Except Chubbs didn't know the half of it. Problem was, neither did I. What the hell was Manny Adonis trying to pull? He knew the kind of guy Scarlo was. Why encourage him to lose more?

"I'll be in the office," Linda said.

I nodded and gave Chubbs a fresh drink. When she was gone, Chubbs said, "That your girl?"

"I'm working on it. Listen, Chubbs, about Adonis."

He raised his hand. "Forget it, Frankie. It's fuckin' history." He hauled himself up, threw a twenty on the bar. "Stay loose, buddy."

He left and I went back to cleaning glasses. It would help me think. I'd barely started when Linda came back.

"I was waiting for him to leave," she said. "Everything all right?"

"I don't know," I said. "How's Rox?"

"Fast asleep."

"That's quite a sister you've got there. A real case."

Linda chuckled. "I'm just happy she's pulling herself together. All she needs now is a break."

"Don't we all?"

"Still worried?"

"You jest," I said, rinsing shotglasses. "Of course I'm worried. The D.A.'s going to call me in any day now. No way I'll ever talk to him."

"Why not?"

"You don't get it, do you? It's not because I don't want to. I'd bury that fat bastard if I could."

"Then do it, Frank. Tell them everything."

"Sure," I said. "And by this time tomorrow I'm playing water polo with Sid and Nick. You're forgetting about Mr. Adonis. Thanks, but I'll pass."

"I don't understand," Linda said. "I mean there's no love lost between Adonis and Betso. You've been saying that all along. Haven't you?"

"You don't have to love a guy to be his partner. Adonis told me he was working on something with Betso. That's why he was so pissed off at what Scarlo pulled, worried he'd blown the deal."

"Now I'm really confused," Linda said. "If that's the case, how come Adonis framed Betso?"

"Who knows? Maybe Betso backed out after the Scarlo thing. Maybe Adonis had it planned all the while. Corporate politics, mob style. It doesn't matter, Linda. I could swear up and down to Adonis that I'd never say a word to the D.A. The fact is I know too much. He couldn't take the chance."

"Oh my God," Linda said. "What about us? We know as much as you do . . . about Scarlo I mean."

I reached over and held Linda's hand. She'd turned the color of milk. I told her not to worry but she trembled anyway. I couldn't blame her.

"Grimm," she said. "We have to tell Grimm."

I shook my head. "He can't help us. Look, maybe you and Rox should get out of here for a while."

"What about you? Here . . . alone."

"I can't go," I said. "My brother owns half of this place. I can't just leave it and run. Besides, Adonis won't come in while the heat's still on. I'll stick around, go through the act—everything normal. Maybe I can buy you some time. Do you have any money?"

"Some. Not much. I'm frightened again, Frank."

"Don't be," I said. "I'll work it out somehow."

"I don't know, I—oh, my God," she said, turning her head toward the door.

I didn't have to look. One look at Linda's face and I knew. Heat or no heat, Adonis was coming in. I turned halfway.

"What's the matter, Frankie? Aren't you glad to see me?"

He was standing in the doorway, his voice drifting out of the shadows. I craned my neck and strained my eyes. Was he alone or was I kidding myself? Adonis never went anywhere by himself. My heart was pounding.

"So," he said, stepping into the light. "Am I welcome or not? Who are you?" he said to Linda.

Linda stammered. "L-L-Linda Dorsey."

"Nice to see you, Linda. You won't mind if Frankie and I have a word or two."

Linda squeezed my hand.

"Right," I said. "Go to my office. I'll be there in a minute. And stay off the phone, I'm expecting a call."

I wasn't expecting a damn thing except trouble. I just wanted Manny to know he shouldn't sweat a panic call to the cops.

Slowly Linda got down from the stool. I couldn't see but I could tell from the look on Manny's face that Linda's skirt had hiked high up her legs. He watched her walk away, nodding appreciatively until we heard the click of my office door.

"Fine looking woman," he said. "And she cares about you. It's important to have a woman who cares. I've been married twenty-two years. Believe me, I know."

I've never known a wiseguy who didn't beat around the bush before passing sentence on his mark. It's a power play, their way of letting you know they're holding a pat hand against your busted flush. They'll ask about your wife's health and one day later make her a widow.

I would have shown more patience but I was fed up with being intimidated.

"Leave her out of this," I said. "She can't hurt you."

He pursed his lips and slowly shook his head. "You're not a bad guy, Fontana. You got guts and you're smart enough to survive. There's only one thing about you I don't like. You keep telling me what to do and think. That's very irritating. Because, you see, you haven't the slightest idea what I do or think. For instance. *You* think I'm here to make trouble." He unbuttoned his white linen sportcoat and held it open. "You see any trouble here? Look around, you see anybody? If you did have trouble with me, it would have been over by now. So give me a J.D. neat and I'll tell you what I really want."

I poured him a shot of Jack Daniels, keeping my back to him so he wouldn't see my hands shaking, then served it up.

"Here's to good fortune," he said. He hoisted the drink to his lips and polished it off. Then he glanced around. "You got a nice place here, Frankie. The guys come in, feel relaxed. That's important, to relax. Have fun. Know what I mean?"

"Fun," I said. "Yeah, I know what you mean."

Adonis lifted his face and gazed off at something only he could

see. "That's what I miss the most. The good times we used to
have. Latin Quarter. Town and Country. The Copa. Class joints.
We'd walk in and take over the place. Sinatra, Durante, Frankie
Laine. They'd send us drinks, for Christ's sake." He shook his
head. "Today it's different. You wanna see Sammy and Frank you
gotta see them in *concert*. In fucking Madison Square Garden. It
kills me to sit there, all those yokels breathing barley soup down
my neck.

"And then, after the show, what's to do, eh? Come to Fontana's
for veal francese? It's nice, but it's not the same. I spent the whole
night once with Joe E. Lewis. Joe E. Lewis! Laughs? Forget
about it. The man was a giant. Now what'a we have? Fast food
joints and discos. It's a damn shame."

I coughed. Adonis twitched. He blinked his eyes and looked at
me. "You heard what happened in Hoboken?"

He'd switched gears so fast that he caught me flat-footed. I
nodded.

"So? What do you think?"

"I think somebody's pretty clever."

"What else?" he said.

"Look, Mr. Adonis, I'm standing here with my guts in a knot. I
don't know if I'm alive or dead. You've got something to say. Get it
out and let's finish this once and for all."

"You're nervous," he said. "That's too bad. But I understand.
All right, here it is. You and the D.A. are going to have a sit
down. He's going to ask you about Betso and Johnny. He's
confused right now. Thinks I'm involved in what happened. You
set him straight. Betso had good reason to hit Johnny. No one
knows that better than you. Tell him what went down at Bally's.
Give him Jake the dealer and that creep Carmine Genovese. He'll
ask about the money and you'll tell him what happened on the

parkway. Make it convincing. Give him the money if you have to. But if I was you, I'd improvise. Know what I mean?"

"Listen," I said, "about the money—"

He raised his hand. "That's your business. I don't want it and Alfie sure doesn't care about it either. Not anymore. With his ass in the can and his crew reshuffling, he's not going to sweat a few hundred grand."

"Wait a minute," I said. "You saying I can keep it?"

"That's up to you and the D.A."

"There's going to be a trial," I said. "I'll have to testify."

"Exactly. Make it good. I want the fat man buried alive. You see, Frankie, there are some guys you can't mess with. That's why I'm lucky. Hell, it's not my fault Betso got busted. It's a coincidence, that's all."

"Everyone knows he was set up."

"There you go again," Adonis said. "Saying what everyone knows. All they know is that Betso's finished. He'll yap and point his fat little finger, but no one'll know who did what. And no one'll care. Least of all his own crew, and especially the guy who's going to run it while Betso's away. He's already talked to the silent partners and everything's okay. He's a friend of mine, Frankie. I trust him. So should you. When he says he'll guarantee your safety, I believe him."

I turned around and stared at the mirror.

"What the hell are you doing?" he said.

"I just wanna see if it's the same guy I shaved this morning."

He laughed. "You never know, do you, Frank?"

He held out his hand and I pumped it like an Ohio pig farmer.

"Well," he said, "I have to run."

"Wait a second," I said. "I'll walk you out."

"That's nice," he said.

I ran around the bar. He waited until I got alongside him. Then he shocked the hell out of me. He threw his arm over my shoulder.

"I'll be following the case in the papers," Adonis said as we walked slowly, casually out of Fontana's. "You should photograph very well. And believe me, it's not going to hurt your business one iota."

A car was waiting for him. The door opened as we approached. "I'll stop in for dinner when things get back to normal," he said.

He got in the back seat. "Oh," he said, leaning out. "Have you heard they may reopen the Copa? Ciao, Frank." The door slammed shut and a second later they pulled away.

Adonis, what a cagey bastard. He had it wired all the way. Scarlo would off Betso sooner or later. All he needed was a little push. Eight ball and the fifteen in the corner pocket. Click click.

I stood there a moment, breathing in the night air. A clean, fresh aroma blew gently off the river. I let the breeze caress my face, clear my mind, as I strolled dreamily toward the great skyline that rose out of the river.